**'I'm going b...
afternoon, and...
me in irons to ...**

'And you think that can't be arranged?' he declared, every bit as angry now as she was.

'Mario, I know you're just trying to protect me, but I *have* to go back to work. You've been a doctor. People *need* me, and I can't let them down. I simply can't.'

'I appreciate that, Kate, I do. But this isn't a game,' he protested.

'The risk is worth taking.'

It wasn't worth taking for him, he thought, as his eyes met hers. If anything should happen to her… If he never saw her laugh again, or smelt her perfume… But he couldn't tell her that, hated admitting it even to himself.

'OK,' he said slowly, 'if you want to go back to work, then I'll let you. But,' he continued as her large grey eyes lit up with clear delight, 'there are conditions. You have to let me come back and work in your department—'

'Not a problem.'

'—and you have to let me move in with you.'

Maggie Kingsley says she can't remember a time when she didn't want to be a writer, but she put her dream on hold and decided to 'be sensible' and become a teacher instead. Five years at the chalk face was enough to convince her she wasn't cut out for it, and she 'escaped' to work for a major charity. Unfortunately—or fortunately!—a back injury ended her career, and when she and her family moved to a remote cottage in the north of Scotland it was her family who nagged her into attempting to make her dream a reality. Combining a love of romantic fiction with a knowledge of medicine gleaned from the many professionals in her family, Maggie says she can't now imagine ever being able to have so much fun legally doing anything else!

Recent titles by the same author:

A CONSULTANT CLAIMS HIS BRIDE
THE GOOD FATHER
THE SURGEON'S MARRIAGE DEMAND

THE CONSULTANT'S ITALIAN KNIGHT

BY
MAGGIE KINGSLEY

All the characters in this book have no existence outside the imagination
of the author, and have no relation whatsoever to anyone bearing the
same name or names. They are not even distantly inspired by any
individual known or unknown to the author, and all the incidents are
pure invention.

First published in Great Britain 2007
Harlequin Mills & Boon Limited,
Eton House, 18-24 Paradise Road, Richmond, Surrey TW9 1SR

© Maggie Kingsley 2007

ISBN-13: 978 0 263 85255 4

Set in Times Roman 10 on 12¼ pt
03-0807-53340

Printed and bound in Spain
by Litografia Rosés, S.A., Barcelona

THE
CONSULTANT'S
ITALIAN KNIGHT

CHAPTER ONE

'BE CAREFUL what you wish for.'

That's what her mother had always said to her when she was a little girl, Kate Kennedy remembered.

'Be careful what you wish for because it might actually come true.'

Well, it had come true, Kate thought, as she gazed out over the crowded waiting room of the A and E department of the General Infirmary in Aberdeen. Three years ago, at the age of thirty-two, she'd become one of the youngest A and E consultants in the country. She'd got the job she'd always wanted, a husband who had loved her, and the perfect home, but now…

'Broken arm in cubicle 4, Kate. Stomach pains in 6, a wheezer in 1, and a seven-year-old with a cut leg in 3.'

Kate turned to see Terri Campbell, the blonde-haired, middle-aged sister in charge of the nursing staff of the A and E department regarding her expectantly, and managed a smile.

'Business as usual, then,' she replied, glancing back at the waiting room in time to see a fight break out between the two young men who had been drinking steadily ever since they'd arrived.

'You OK, Kate?'

Concern had replaced the expectant look on Terri's face, and Kate forced her smile back into place.

'Bad attack of Saturday night blues,' she lied. 'Everyone else is out there enjoying themselves, and I'm stuck in here, on a hot August evening, tending to the ungrateful, the ungracious and the just plain stupid.'

'Yes, but you wouldn't want it any other way, would you?' The sister laughed.

Once upon a time she wouldn't have, Kate thought, but now she was beginning to wonder whether the price she'd had to pay for achieving her dream had been too high. Way too high.

'Are you *sure* you're OK, Kate?'

Terri was frowning at her now and, for a second, Kate hesitated, but she and the unit sister had been friends for the past three years and she knew she'd have to tell her eventually.

'It came this morning,' she said with an effort. 'My decree nisi.'

'Oh, Kate—'

'It's not like it was unexpected,' Kate interrupted, not wanting the sister's sympathy, knowing she couldn't deal with it right now. 'We both knew there was no way back when John left me last year, but I sort of thought…' She sighed and shook her head. 'I don't know what I thought. Maybe that the decree nisi would be bigger, more impressive, but it was just an ordinary piece of paper. Not much to show for six years of marriage. Five years if you don't count the year John and I were separated, and I don't suppose I should.'

Terri stared at her helplessly. 'Kate, I'm so sorry. I hoped there might be a chance of you and John getting back together again.'

'He's found somebody else,' Kate said. 'He told me last week. Her name's Sandy. She weighs seven stone including her hair extensions, and she's a fashion buyer.'

'Oh. Right.' Terri bit her lip, then pushed her glasses firmly up the bridge of her nose. 'Well, at least some good might come out of this.'

'Some *good?*' Kate repeated faintly, and Terri nodded.

'If she's a fashion buyer maybe she'll be able to talk him out of those God-awful black suits and button down shirts he *will* persist in wearing. The ones which make him resemble a third-rate undertaker.'

Kate stared speechlessly at the sister for a second, then burst out laughing.

'Oh, Terri, what would I do without you?' she exclaimed, and the sister grinned.

'Be even loopier than you already are?' she suggested. 'Seriously, if I can help at all—if you want to scream or yell or just generally vent—I'm here for you.'

Did she want to scream and yell? Kate wondered. Did she really?

She might feel hurt, and confused, and not a little bewildered, but if she was honest with herself—and Kate fully intended to be honest—she didn't want John back. They'd fallen out of love a long time ago.

'I'm fine, Terri,' she declared. 'Truly I am.'

'Well, the offer's there if you should ever want it,' Terri said. 'Lord knows, you've listened to my worries about my son more times than I care to remember.'

'Neil will be OK, Terri—I know he will,' Kate said gently. 'He's only eighteen, and we all make stupid mistakes at that age, but he's got you and Frank, and now this new job. He's beginning to turn his life around.'

'I hope so, but working in a bar… It's not what I imagined for him,' Terri said unhappily. 'He was—is—such a clever boy, and if he hadn't got in with the wrong crowd at school… Frank says the bar work will do him good, make him stand on his own two feet, but…'

'Terri, he'll be fine,' Kate insisted. 'He *will*.'

'And so will you,' the sister said, clearly deliberately changing the subject. 'There's somebody out there who's just right for you, I know there is.'

'I don't want to meet anybody else,' Kate said firmly. 'One failed marriage is quite enough for me.'

'Kate, you're only thirty-four—'

'Thirty-five at the beginning of next month,' Kate reminded her.

'—and just because it didn't work out with John,' Terri continued determinedly, 'doesn't mean it won't work out with somebody else. For all you know, Mr Right could be just about to walk through that door this very minute, and change your life completely.'

Not Mr Right, but Mr Never-in-a-Million-Years, Kate thought, with a shaky inward chuckle, as Terri sped across to their receptionist to see why she was waving frantically at her and the door of the waiting room opened and two men appeared.

The younger of the two men was tall, in his early thirties, with neat blond hair and a frank, open face, but his companion…

Intimidating. That was the only word that could adequately describe him, Kate decided, and it wasn't just because he was considerably taller and more muscular than his companion. It wasn't even because his thick black hair brushed the neck of an ancient brown leather jacket, or his denims were faded and worn, or even that he was wearing a pair of the scruffiest trainers she'd ever seen. It was his face.

Darker skinned than the average Aberdonian, she would have guessed him to be Spanish, or Italian, if it hadn't been for his eyes. Cobalt-blue eyes. Piercing blue eyes that stared back at her with neither warmth nor gentleness, but only a world-weary cynicism that said all too plainly, Don't mess with me.

'MVA on the way,' Terri declared as she rejoined her. 'Single car hit the crash barrier on the motorway, broken tib and fib, and suspected internal bleeding. Oh, and you're going to love this,' she added, her expression clearly suggesting otherwise. 'We've also got a young man coming in from Aberdeen airport. He collapsed just after he came through Customs, and the security guys suspect he's a body-packer.'

Kate groaned inwardly. That was all she needed this evening. If the young man *was* a body-packer then his collapse suggested that one of his packets had burst, and the only other body-packer she had ever treated had died. Swiftly, and extremely painfully.

'OK, make sure we've plenty of house red for the MVA,' she declared. 'As for the body-packer… Let's hope he's simply an innocent traveller who's had a heart attack.'

And the man in the waiting room was still staring at her, she noticed as she turned to go back into the treatment room. Staring, and smiling. Not at her, she realised, but at something his companion had said, but that smile… Just for a second it completely softened his face, making him heart-clutchingly attractive. He was still as intimidating as hell, of course, but that smile… Yup, it definitely pushed all of her buttons and, unconsciously, her fingers went up to the hair clips which were spectacularly failing to keep her shoulder-length, auburn hair back in a neat chignon.

Getting her hair restyled was on her 'to do' list. So was losing some weight and buying more furniture for the ground floor flat she'd moved into when she and John had separated. The flat that depressed the hell out of her every time she opened the front door, but why she should suddenly find herself thinking about that, and her hair, and losing some weight, just because an attractive—OK, make that very attractive—man was sitting in the waiting room was beyond her.

'Kate?'

Terri was still waiting for her, and Kate squared her shoulders firmly.

The man was just a man. Someone she'd probably never see again, and that was exactly the way she wanted it. No more relationships, no more heartbreak, plus the likelihood of somebody like him ever being interested in someone like her was nil, she thought wryly, as she began to walk towards the treatment room door. No man who looked as good as he did when he smiled would ever be interested in an overweight little woman like her.

Which was just as well, she told herself, as she risked a quick glance over her shoulder and saw he was still watching her. Relationships might be fraught with uncertainty and danger at the best of times, but this man already had danger written all over him.

'I thought he'd be here by now,' Ralph Evanton declared, dragging his fingers impatiently through his blond hair as he sat down on one of the waiting room chairs. 'According to our info, the ambulance picked him up ten minutes ago.'

'It's Saturday night,' Mario Volante replied. 'The traffic will be heavy.'

'I suppose so.' Ralph glanced round, then lowered his voice. 'Do you reckon he's still alive?'

'If the ambulance comes in with its siren blaring, he's alive. If it doesn't…' Mario pulled over one of the battered waiting room chairs and sat down, too. 'Either way—alive or DOA—we'll know soon enough.'

'You'd think they'd realise it was a mug's game, wouldn't you?' Ralph observed. 'That what they're buying into can all too quickly become a one-way ticket to the Big Guy upstairs.'

Mario shrugged. 'Life's tough. It's even tougher if you're stupid.'

Ralph stared at him silently for a moment, then cleared his throat. 'You know, you can be a complete and utter bastard at times.'

'I prefer to call myself a realist.'

'Yeah. Right.'

Absently, Ralph drummed his fingers against the side of his chair, then pulled his mobile phone out of his jacket only to swiftly pocket it when Mario nudged him and gestured towards the sign on the waiting room wall reminding all visitors that mobile phones must be switched off within the hospital confines.

'Oughtn't we to at least introduce ourselves to that woman on Reception?' Ralph demanded. 'Tell her why we're here?'

'The fewer people who know who we are, the better.'

'I guess so.' Ralph turned in his seat as the waiting room door opened, and grimaced as a girl with a badly cut knee limped in. 'I hate hospitals.'

'Really?' A glimmer of a smile creased Mario Volante's lips. 'I never would have guessed. Look, will you relax?' he continued as Ralph opened his mouth to protest. 'I'm trying very hard not to draw attention to myself, but you're squirming around as though you've sat on something.'

'Sorry. I just—'

'Hate hospitals,' Mario finished for him, his smile widening. 'Yeah, so you said.'

'It looks like something might be happening,' Ralph declared, sitting up straighter in his seat and nodding in the direction of the reception desk. 'That blonde-haired nurse with the glasses looks worried, and so does the pretty little nurse with the auburn hair.'

'The chubby, auburn-haired one is a doctor not a nurse.'

'Mario, she only looks chubby to you because you usually date toothpicks,' Ralph protested. 'To me she looks like a real woman. A woman with her curves in all the right places.'

'And does Jenny know you're looking at other women and deciding whether they have their curves in all the right places?' Mario said with a quizzical glance.

Ralph looked smug. 'My wife trusts me.'

'Uh-huh. Plus, I distinctly remember her saying at your wedding that if you ever cheated on her she'd nail your butt to the wall and use it as a dartboard.'

'She did, too,' Ralph said with a splutter of laughter. 'But I stand by what I said. That girl has all her curves in the right places, and she's pretty, too.'

But not happy, Mario decided as he stared across at the

auburn-haired girl. In his work it was his job to read people, and this girl—woman—was definitely not happy. There were shadows under her large grey eyes, and her face was white and drawn as though she hadn't been sleeping well recently.

'That's what you need,' Ralph observed, seeing the direction of his gaze. 'A good woman in your life.'

'And just when did this paragon become not just a real woman, but also a good one?' Mario protested, and Ralph shook his head, clearly amazed at the question.

'She's a doctor, Mario. It stands to reason she'll be the caring, nurturing type.'

With a backbone of steel if he was any judge of character, Mario decided as he watched the auburn-haired doctor reply to something the nurse had said. Medicine was a tough profession for a woman, and for this woman to work in A and E she had to be no pushover, and from the stubborn tilt of her jaw he knew she wasn't.

'What you need is some stability in your life, Mario,' Ralph continued, 'starting with a proper, grown-up relationship.'

'You'll be trying to fix me up with your kid sister next,' Mario said dryly. 'Or your cousin from Glasgow.'

'I wouldn't trust you with either of them, but that girl looks as though she could handle you.'

'You think I need handling?' Mario declared, amusement plain on his face, and Ralph raised an eyebrow.

'Mario, you discard women with as little thought as you change your socks. Now, that girl—'

'Enough, Ralph,' Mario interrupted, his patience clearly at an end. 'I'm not interested.'

'Then you *should* be,' Ralph insisted. 'Hell, mate, you've been divorced for four years, and, OK, so divorce is never pleasant and Sue hurt you badly, but it's time you moved on, time you buried the hurt.'

He would have done, Mario thought grimly, if Sue really had hurt him, but the trouble was she hadn't. If she had hurt him he would at least have known he was still able to feel, to care, but when she'd left all he'd felt was an overwhelming sense of relief that the arguing was finally over.

'Mario, listen to me—'

'Madre di Dio!' Mario exclaimed, and Ralph held up his hands in defeat.

'OK—OK. When you start speaking Italian I know it's time to shut up. You're happy as you are. Fine. Great.'

And he was happy, Mario thought as he watched the auburn-haired doctor fiddle with her hair. Lovely hair it was, too. The kind of hair that should never be tied back but allowed to flow loose and free, and Ralph had been right about the curves. They were definitely in all the right places, but he wasn't interested. He had a job that he loved, the career he'd always wanted, and it was enough for him. OK, so there were times when he was lonely, but if he'd been looking for a new relationship—and he wasn't—the girl standing at the reception desk wasn't for him. He preferred his women quiet, placid and accommodating, and he suspected the auburn-haired doctor was anything but.

'Sounds like it might be show time,' Ralph declared as the distant wail of a siren split the air.

It did indeed, Mario thought, as he saw the nurse and the auburn-haired doctor disappear back into the treatment room. It also meant their man was still alive, and with a sigh he stretched out his long, denim clad legs. It was going to be a long night.

'According to his passport, his name's Duncan Hamilton, and he's nineteen years old,' one of the paramedics declared, desperately trying to restrain the arms and legs of the young man who was thrashing about wildly on the trolley. 'When security at the airport said they suspected he might be a body-packer, we just bagged him, and did a scoop and run.'

'Symptoms?' Kate asked.

'Severe agitation, BP 160 over 90 and rising and he started fitting just as we pulled up outside.'

Kate bit her lip. Absorption of large amounts of cocaine caused agitation, hypertension and seizures, but Duncan Hamilton's symptoms could be due to other conditions, too. If she knew for certain that it wasn't a leaking cocaine packet she would immediately have started him on naloxone, but the drug would have no effect on a patient suffering from a massive overdose.

'Did he have anything else on him apart from his passport?' she asked hopefully. 'Maybe a medic alert disc detailing a pre-existing medical condition?'

The paramedic shook his head, and Kate swore under her breath.

If Duncan Hamilton was a body-packer then it certainly sounded as though one of his packets had burst, but she needed more than a suspicion. She needed certainty.

'Mr Hamilton—Duncan,' she said, leaning as far over the young man as his writhing body would allow. 'Do you know where you are, and what's happening to you?'

A low moan was her only reply, and she gave up on the preliminaries and went for the straight approach.

'Duncan, how many packets of cocaine did you swallow?'

'I didn't… I haven't swallowed anything,' the young man gasped as Terri finished cutting off his clothes and began placing plastic suckers on his chest to link him to the heart monitor.

'Duncan, if one of your packets has burst you could die,' Kate persisted, 'so tell me the truth. How many did you swallow?'

For a moment she didn't think he was going to answer, then he muttered, 'Hundred. Swallowed a hundred.'

Hell-fire, and damnation. The average lethal dose of cocaine hydrochloride was 500 milligrams. Body-packers commonly swallowed packets containing at least 12 grams each, and Duncan Hamilton said he'd swallowed a hundred of them. If just one of them had burst then more than twenty-four times the lethal dosage was seeping into his body, affecting his central nervous system, and respiratory and cardiovascular systems.

'OK, Terri, we need to calm him and cool him down fast!' she exclaimed as the paramedics wheeled their stretcher out of the cubicle. 'I want 5 milligrams midazolam, supplemental oxygen, his head, neck and chest kept cold with cold water, and can you get me a fan? If we can control his agitation and temperature we might be able to get his BP down. If not…'

The sister's eyes met hers, and Kate knew what Terri was thinking. Duncan Hamilton could code at any minute, and with so much cocaine travelling through his body the chances of pulling him back were slim.

'I'll get the fan,' Terri said but, to Kate's dismay, the minute the sister had gone Duncan Hamilton wrenched the ambu-bag from his face.

'Need to…tell you something,' he said, his breath coming in great, ragged gulps.

'Later—you can tell me later,' Kate declared, desperately trying to get the ambu-bag back in place but he fought her all the way.

'Important!' he exclaimed, grasping her wrist tightly. 'Have to tell you. Names… Important names. Bolton…Faranelli—'

'Duncan, will you please let me put this back on you,' Kate insisted, seeing the heart monitor starting to display an increasingly erratic tracing.

'Mackay… Di Angelis… And addresses—I have addresses. You *must* hear the addresses.'

'OK—OK, I'm listening,' Kate replied, hoping that the quicker the young man told her whatever he wanted so desperately to tell her, the sooner she might be able to re-affix the ambu-bag.

'6 Mount Stewart Street… 12 Picard Avenue…'

Oh, *shut up*, Kate thought as Duncan rambled on and she scarcely listened. He was dying, and yet he was giving her what sounded like the entire contents of the telephone directory.

'Did…did you get all that?' Duncan Hamilton demanded eventually, and Kate nodded.

'Absolutely,' she lied, sighing with relief as she snapped the ambu-bag back in place, but neither it, nor the fan Terri brought, nor the sedation, reduced Duncan Hamilton's soaring temperature.

'If we don't get his temperature down soon he's going to develop hypothermia,' Terri declared, worry plain in her voice. 'Will I start him on lidocaine?'

'It won't help,' Kate replied, no less concerned than the sister was. 'It produces similar effects on the myocardial cell membrane to cocaine. I've used sodium bicarbonate for tricyclic antidepressant overdoses and it worked with them so maybe…'

She didn't get a chance to finish what she'd been about to say. Duncan Hamilton suddenly gave an odd breath, and the heart monitor let out a low and constant tone. He'd coded, and immediately Kate hit him squarely in the centre of his sternum, then glanced across at the monitor. Nothing. No change. The heart line remained resolutely flat.

'Paddles, Terri!' she exclaimed.

Swiftly, the sister handed them to her, and equally quickly, Kate rubbed the defibrillating paddles together with electrical conducting gel. It was on occasions like this she wished she was six feet tall instead of five feet nothing. To successfully shock a patient you had to lean over the examination trolley, place the paddles in exactly the right place, then press down really hard, but the trolleys had metal rails and if any part of you touched them…

'Instant cardiac arrest, Kate,' she muttered, standing as high on her toes as she could. 'Stand clear, Terri!'

The sister stepped back from the trolley, Kate pressed the

paddles down as hard as she could on either side of Duncan Hamilton's chest, and he convulsed briefly.

'Nothing,' Terri said, her voice tense.

'I'll tube him,' Kate declared. 'The ambu-bag's not enough any more, so I'll tube him and then I want the power up to 300.'

Terri waited until Kate had inserted an endotracheal tube down Duncan Hamilton's throat, then upped the power on the defibrillator paddles to 300, but though Duncan Hamilton's body convulsed again when Kate placed the paddles on either side of his chest the monitor reading didn't change.

'IV bolus of 500 milligrams of beryllium,' Kate said in desperation. 'Power up to 360 joules.'

Again, and again, she placed the defibrillator paddles on either side of the young man's chest, but no amount of electricity kick-started the young man's heart and eventually she stepped back from the trolley, and switched off the current.

'You did your best, Kate,' Terri declared, watching her. 'It's just…'

'This time we didn't win.' Kate's eyes clouded. 'I know.'

'Look, why don't you take a break, grab yourself a cup of coffee?' the sister suggested. 'I'll clear up in here for you.'

'Thanks,' Kate replied. 'I just want…'

'A few minutes alone with him,' Terri finished for her. 'I understand.'

And Terri did, Kate thought. The sister knew how much she hated losing a patient—any patient—and this man was so young. Nineteen, the paramedic had said. Nineteen, and his whole life should have been ahead of him, but now…

Tears pricked at the back of her eyes, and desperately she tried to blink them away. It wasn't like her to break down like this, and if the other consultants at the hospital could see her they'd have a field day.

'Head of A and E isn't a suitable position for a woman,' they'd whispered when she'd got the job three years ago. 'And thirty-two's far too young.'

Maybe they'd been right, she thought as she gently closed Duncan Hamilton's eyes, and whispered, 'I'm sorry—so sorry,' as she always did when she lost a patient. Maybe if she hadn't been quite so driven, quite so determined to prove she was up to the job, but the glossy magazines had said she could have it all, and she'd believed them.

She'd kept on believing them even when John had started muttering that he hardly ever saw her. She hadn't even worried when he'd begun booking himself on seminars without talking to her about them first, but her morning's post had burst her illusory bubble once and for all. You couldn't have it all. Or, at least, she couldn't.

'Did you forget something, Terri?' she said, wiping her eyes quickly with the back of her hand as she heard the sound of the cubicle curtains opening behind her.

'I'm not Terri.'

He wasn't. He was the dark-haired, olive-skinned man from the waiting room and, as he advanced towards her, she wondered why she had ever thought him attractive. Up close, with a two-day stubble that wouldn't have looked out of place on a convict, and a good sixteen inches taller than she was, he looked even more intimidating than he had at a distance.

'I'm sorry, but we don't allow friends or family members into this part of A and E,' she said with a calmness she was very far from feeling. 'If you'd care to wait outside—'

'I'm not a friend or family.'

That didn't surprise her. In fact, she had a sudden horrifying suspicion that he was probably the man who had put Duncan Hamilton into A and E in the first place.

'If you're not a friend, or family, you'll definitely have to wait outside,' she said. 'Somebody—' hopefully not her '—will be able to give you an update on Mr Hamilton's condition in a few minutes.'

The man glanced down at Duncan Hamilton.

'Not much need of an update when he's rather obviously dead,' he said. 'What I'm more interested in is what he might have said to you before he died.'

That didn't sound good, and neither did the way this man was looking at her.

'We don't give out information to non-relatives,' she declared, 'so will you please go back to the waiting room.'

He didn't look as though he was going to. In fact, a look of distinct irritation appeared on his face and, as he reached inside his leather jacket, every police drama she had ever seen on TV suddenly flashed into her mind.

He was going to kill her. He was Duncan Hamilton's fixer, or agent, and though his accent was surprisingly Scottish he was probably a member of the Mafia as well, and he was going to kill her.

But that didn't mean she had to give in without a fight, she decided.

'OK, I've tried polite!' she exclaimed, snatching a syringe from the instrument trolley beside her, 'but polite is clearly something you don't understand. This syringe contains a sample of your friend's blood and if I'm not very much mistaken he's probably HIV positive. Come one step closer to me and you're going to be HIV positive, too.'

He glanced down at the syringe, then at her. 'That syringe is empty.'

Damn, and blast, but she'd picked up the wrong one.

'It's…plasma.' She bluffed. 'Plasma is a part of blood, but it has no colour—'

'Lady, that syringe is empty, and I am…' He reached inside his jacket again, and she closed her eyes.

This was it. She was dead, finished, history, and she could see the newspaper headlines now.

Forty-five-year-old, divorced female consultant…because the newspapers always got your age wrong…*murdered at the General Infirmary. Ms Kate Kennedy was found lying in a pool of blood having been shot at close range by—*

'…Inspector Mario Volante.'

Her eyes flew open to see the man was holding out a police identity badge towards her and felt more foolish than she'd ever done in her life.

'You're a policeman,' she said faintly. 'But you…'

Quickly she bit off the rest of what she'd been about to say. Maybe he was undercover, and it was part of his brief to look scruffy. And then again, maybe she was just an idiot.

'You thought I was some sort of hit man, didn't you?' he said, his mouth twitching into a smile, and she flushed.

'What else was I supposed to think?' she demanded. 'You appear out of nowhere, looking like…'

'Like what?' he said, clearly confused, and the colour on her cheeks darkened.

'The way you're dressed… All the policemen I've ever seen have worn uniforms, with caps, and badges, and…and stuff.'

'I'm CID, Drugs Squad, as is my colleague, Detective Sergeant Evanton. We don't go in for uniforms, and caps, and badges, and…stuff.'

He was laughing at her. She knew he was, and nobody—but nobody—laughed at Kate Kennedy.

'You don't sound Italian, Inspector Volante,' she said tersely, and his eyebrows rose.

'I was born in Aberdeen to an Italian father and a Scottish mother, but even if both my parents had been Italian that doesn't mean I have to sound like I'm auditioning for a part in *The Godfather.*'

It was a rebuke, and a just one. It also, she thought, explained his amazingly blue eyes.

'Let's cut to the chase, Inspector Volante,' she declared, tossing the syringe back onto the instrument trolley. 'As you so correctly noticed, Mr Hamilton is dead, so neither you nor your colleague is going to get any information out of him.'

'Did he say anything to you before he died?'

'Just some names and addresses—nothing that made any sense—and now, if you'll excuse me, I have a waiting room full of sick people—'

'I want to hear what he said.'

'And didn't you hear what *I* said?' she exclaimed. 'It was just a random list of names, and addresses, and I'm busy. B-U-S-Y.'

He squinted at her name tag.

'Dr Kennedy, I'm busy, too,' he said, his tone even, 'and if you don't give me ten minutes of your time I'll take you downtown and book you for obstruction and, believe me, that will take a whole lot longer than ten minutes particularly if we include the strip search.'

He meant it. She could tell from the cold, hard gleam in his blue eyes that he meant it, and she gritted her teeth.

'OK. All I can remember him saying—'

'Not here,' he interrupted. 'I want somewhere quiet— private—where we can't be overheard. What's through there?' he added, nodding at the door at the end of the treatment room.

'A store cupboard.'

'Perfect.'

Not for her, it wasn't, Kate thought, as Mario Volante steered her into the cupboard and shut the door. If she'd thought he was big and intimidating in the treatment room, it was as nothing to how big and intimidating he felt when he was standing toe to toe with her in a cupboard.

'Cosy, isn't it?' he said, as though he'd read her mind, and her chin came up.

He was laughing at her again—she knew he was—and she'd had enough of him laughing at her. More than enough.

'Look, can we get on with this?' she demanded.

'Fine by me,' he said, extracting a small black notebook from his pocket and elbowing her in the ribs in the process. 'OK, tell me exactly what Hamilton said.'

With an effort she forced herself to think of nothing but the few minutes she'd spent alone with Duncan Hamilton.

'First he told me some names. Di Angelis was one, and Mackay was another. Fascali—' She frowned. 'No, that's not right. Faranelli. Yes, that was it. Faranelli.'

'Any other names?' he said, his pen flashing across the page of his notebook.

'There was one more. It was the name of a town, but...' She thought hard, and eventually shook her head. 'I'm sorry, it's gone.'

'Don't worry about it. It might come back to you later. Tell me the addresses.'

'Inspector Volante,' she protested. 'Duncan Hamilton had pulled off his ambu-bag, and I was trying to get it back on again so I wasn't really listening.'

'Please,' he insisted. 'Anything you can tell me—anything at all—might be vitally important.'

His blue eyes were fixed on her, searching, intent, and she swallowed hard. Concentrate, Kate. *Concentrate.*

He has beautiful eyes.

No, not on that. Concentrate on remembering what Duncan Hamilton told you.

'He mentioned a house in Mount Stewart Street,' she said quickly. 'Number 6, I think. And somewhere in Lansdowne Drive. Number 4—or maybe it was number 5. Then there was 55 Cedar Way, and somewhere in Picard Avenue, and...' She shook her head. 'I'm sorry, I can't remember any more.'

'You've done very well,' he replied, snapping shut his notebook.

'I just wish I could have saved Duncan Hamilton's life,' she murmured.

'Once a packet bursts, it's odds on that the body-packer will die.'

'Then why in the world would anyone choose to do it?' she protested, and he shrugged.

'Because money can be a very powerful persuader if you're poor and up to your eyeballs in debt.'

'Yes, but—'

'And they don't all do it for the money,' he continued. 'Some of them are offered safe passage into a country that wouldn't take them if they tried the legal, immigration route, and others do it because their family members are being held as collateral to ensure their cooperation.'

'But that's blackmail,' she gasped, and he smiled a smile that held no warmth at all.

'Welcome to the twenty-first century, Doctor.'

'Are you always this cynical?' she exclaimed before she could stop herself, and his eyebrows rose.

'No, I'm not. According to a very reliable source, I'm also occasionally a complete and utter bastard.'

'Then maybe it's time you got out more,' she said, not bothering to hide her sarcasm. 'Opened your eyes, smelt the flowers, and saw what a beautiful world this can be.'

'Despite all the wars, famines, drugs, unnecessary deaths and diseases?' he observed.

'Despite even that,' she said stoutly, and to her surprise he smiled again, but this time it was the smile which completely softened his face.

The smile which stupidly—ridiculously—made her wish she'd made time for that hairdresser's appointment, lost some weight, maybe even bought herself a new blouse. Something pretty, feminine, and…

She really had to get a grip. Good grief, her divorce had only just come through this morning, and just because this man was standing close to her—so very close—and smiling that smile…

He was probably married, with umpteen kids, and, even if he wasn't one look at him should have been enough to tell her she'd be toast if she ever got involved with him.

'Look, can we get out of this cupboard now?' she exclaimed.

'What?'

'This cupboard—I don't think we need to be in here any more, do you?'

'Probably not, but I was kind of beginning to enjoy it.'

He was also enjoying wrong-footing her, she realised, seeing the glint of laughter in his blue eyes, but she wasn't going to play. Not when she had the very decided feeling that she would lose.

'If there's nothing else, I really do have to get back to work,' she said, reaching for the door handle only to feel an annoying jolt of sensation as her arm brushed across his chest.

'There's just a couple more things,' he replied. 'I'd prefer it if you didn't tell anybody what you've told me, and I'd also prefer it if you didn't tell your colleagues that Ralph Evanton and I are policemen. The fewer people who know anything about what happened here tonight the better.'

'That's fine by me,' she said but, as she opened the cupboard door, and squeezed past him, her heart sank.

Terri was standing outside in the treatment room, and it was all too obvious from the look on her face that she'd got completely the wrong idea of what she and Inspector Volante might have been getting up to in the cupboard.

'Terri, this is…'

Kate came to a halt. If she was not supposed to say who he was, then how on earth was she supposed to introduce him?

'I'm Mario Volante,' he declared, coming to her rescue. 'An old friend of Dr Kennedy's. A *very* old friend.'

He'd said that deliberately, Kate thought angrily, seeing Terri's eyes glance from her to Mario avidly. He'd said that on purpose, knowing full well that she wouldn't—couldn't—contradict him, but she wasn't about to let him get away with it.

'Shouldn't you be going?' she said sweetly. 'You don't want to be late for your over forties reunion.'

'Oh, nice one,' Mario said, his face lighting up with genuine amusement. 'She's just kidding,' he continued, flashing a smile across at Terri. 'She knows very well that I'm only thirty-eight, but she's right about me having to go.'

'Must you?' Terri protested, and he nodded.

'Afraid so. See you around, Kate,' he added, and before she could reply he'd gone.

'Wow, and double wow!' Terri exclaimed. 'Where have you been hiding him?'

'He's a friend of mine from…from med school,' Kate replied, improvising wildly. 'I haven't seen him for years.'

'So, you two aren't an item, then?'

'No, we're not,' Kate said firmly, and Terri looked disappointed.

'Pity,' she murmured.

Not from where I'm standing, it isn't, Kate thought as her pager went off, and she reached into her white coat to answer it. OK, so she couldn't deny that every time Mario Volante had smiled that particular smile she'd felt odd, and hot, and totally unlike herself, but he was also rude, opinionated and arrogant, and any one of those three traits was a complete turn-off. Plus, he was also probably married, which made him a complete louse for chatting up strange women in cupboards.

'You'll never see him again, Kate,' she murmured as she walked down the treatment room, 'and you should thank your lucky stars you won't.'

'Did you manage to get anything out of the receptionist?' Mario asked, pulling the parking ticket off his car windscreen, and tossing it indifferently onto the road.

'Just the standard you're-not-next-of-kin garbage,' Ralph replied as he got into the car. 'The one thing I did find out, though, was that your auburn-haired doctor is the consultant.'

'Kate Kennedy's head of A and E?' Mario frowned. 'Bright lady.'

'Pretty, too,' Ralph declared, shooting Mario a meaningful glance, but Mario ignored him.

'Take a look at this,' he said instead, extracting his notebook from his pocket and throwing it into Ralph's lap. 'Hamilton died before I could speak to him, but he told Dr Kennedy some very interesting things.'

'Interesting?' Ralph repeated as he read through the pages. 'Mario, this is dynamite. Did you tell Dr Kennedy that what she heard could send down three of the biggest drug dealers in Aberdeen for a very long stretch, plus identify possible drug outlets?'

'It's better she doesn't know,' Mario said. 'It's better nobody knows for the moment.'

'You think she'll keep her mouth shut?'

'I told her to, so we can but hope.'

'Then, if your conversation with her was private—and I'm sure it was,' Ralph declared, 'we should be OK.'

Mario had a flashback recollection of himself crushed up against Kate Kennedy in the store cupboard, of her hair smelling of flowers and hot summer evenings, and her full breasts gently rising and falling against his arm, and stamped on the image immediately.

'The trouble is, her conversation with Hamilton wasn't private,' he observed. 'Hospital cubicle curtains are notoriously thin, and you know as well as I do that the fixers have their spies everywhere which means I'm going to have to keep an eye on Dr Kennedy.'

'Purely professionally, of course,' Ralph said slyly, and Mario gave him a hard stare.

For sure, it had been fun to keep wrong-footing Kate Kennedy, and to watch her large grey eyes grow more and more flustered by the minute, but it had just been a bit of fun at the end of a long and tiring day. He had no intention of taking it further. Not personally at any rate.

'Ralph, all I want from Kate Kennedy is facts, and I want them while she's still alive to give them to me.'

'You think our lady doctor could be in trouble?' Ralph asked as they pulled away from the kerb.

Mario executed a fast U-turn in front of the hospital, completely ignoring the angry cacophony of car horns that greeted his manoeuvre, and nodded.

'Yup, I do.'

CHAPTER TWO

'HE'S' back,' Terri said.

'That's nice,' Kate murmured vaguely, more intent on inserting the final suture into the badly cut hand of the young woman sitting in front of her than on what the sister had just said. 'OK,' she continued, straightening up, 'I think that should do it.'

'Will my hand be scarred?' the young woman asked. 'Not that it matters, of course, but…'

'I'm afraid you're going to be left with a couple of faint white lines once those cuts heal,' Kate admitted, 'but, considering what you fell on, it could have been a lot worse. A few centimetres higher, and you would have cut an artery.'

'That'll teach me to pay proper attention when I'm carrying bottles of wine out to a barbecue,' the young woman said with feeling, and Kate chuckled.

'Get some brawny man to do it for you in future. They like looking macho.'

The young woman laughed. 'I'll remember that. Do you want me to come back to get the stitches out?' she added, and Kate shook her head.

'Your own GP can remove them for you, but don't forget to call in at the hospital pharmacy before you leave to collect some painkillers. Once the anaesthetic wears off, I'm afraid your hand is going to feel as though somebody's been inserting red hot needles into it.'

The woman rolled her eyes. 'I'm definitely going to get some brawny man to carry the wine in future,' she declared but, the minute she had gone, Terri cleared her throat discreetly.

'I said, your friend's back.'

'What friend?' Kate asked, rotating her neck wearily, then pulling off her bloodstained surgical gloves and binning them.

'Mario Volante.'

He was *back?* But she still hadn't remembered the fourth name that Duncan Hamilton had given her on Saturday night, and Mario Volante must know she wasn't likely to remember it two days later. Plus, she'd had a long afternoon. A very long afternoon.

Not to mention the fact that you never wanted to see him again, a little voice whispered at the back of her head.

Too darned right, I don't, she thought. He's too unsettling, too aggravating, too everything.

'Tell him I'm sorry, but I don't have time to talk to him right now,' she declared. 'If he'd like to phone—'

'He said you'd say that,' Terri interrupted, 'so he also said to tell you…' The sister's eyes danced. 'That the strip search offer was still on.'

'Oh, did he,' Kate said grimly. 'Well, we'll see about that. Where is he?'

'The waiting room.'

But he wasn't. When Kate marched out of the treatment room, fully intending to give Mario Volante a very large piece of her mind, he was walking down the corridor towards her looking every bit as scruffy and unkempt as he had on Saturday night.

'Don't you own a suit?' she demanded. 'Or at the very least something that doesn't make you look like the people you're supposed to be arresting?'

'Well, hello, and it's nice to see you again, too,' he said, a maddening smile tugging at the corner of his mouth. 'Are you always this cranky?'

'Only when people seem determined to waste my time,' she replied irritably. 'Look, much as I want to help, you already know everything I do, so why don't you just run along and do some really important police work like arresting some little old ladies for jaywalking?'

'I'm back because I need your signature on a transcript.'

'Oh.' Suddenly she felt stupid and, if there was one thing she hated, it was feeling stupid. 'Of course I'll sign—'

'Plus, I have some photographs I want you to look at,' he interrupted. 'They're of people you might have noticed hanging around the waiting room the night Hamilton died, or perhaps since then.'

She gazed up at him, hardly able to believe her ears. 'Inspector Volante—'

'It's Mario.'

'Whatever,' she said dismissively. 'Do you honestly think I have time to run out into the waiting room and stare at who's sitting there?'

'You might recognise somebody.'

'I won't.'

'You might.'

'I *won't*,' she insisted, and he sighed.

'Dr Kennedy, I've had a long day, and I really want to get back to my office before midnight, so we can do this the easy way, or…?'

She stared up into his resolute face. That he was not going to take no for an answer was plain, and if she kept on refusing he'd probably make good on his threat to take her down to the police station and that would be an even bigger waste of her time.

'OK, let's get this over with!' she exclaimed. 'Give me the transcript to sign and then I'll look at your damned photographs.'

He glanced over his shoulder. 'Not here. It's too open, too exposed, and somebody might overhear us.'

'I'm not getting into a cupboard with you again,' she said quickly, and his blue eyes glinted.

'Spoilsport.'

She gritted her teeth. 'Inspector Volante—'

'It's Mario, remember?'

'OK, *Mario*,' she said. 'Look, I'm having a bad day…' *Bad day, bad week, bad year.* '…and I really don't have time for this.'

'Time for what?' he said, all *faux* innocence, and she let out a huff of frustration.

He was winding her up again, she knew he was, and she didn't know who she was angrier with—herself, or him. Why couldn't she effectively silence this infuriating man? She'd never had any trouble in the past. She'd always been able to inflict a crushing snub or a biting retort on anyone who dared suggest she was anything but a doctor first, and a woman second. Why was she so apparently incapable of making that clear now?

Because she didn't want to completely shut him up, she realised as she gazed at him and saw the glint of laughter in his deep blue eyes. Because when he wasn't infuriating her, it was fun to spar with him, and she had to stop thinking it was fun or she was going to be in big trouble.

'My office is down that corridor,' she said frostily. 'We'll use that.'

'Terrific,' he said, and strode off without even waiting for her to lead the way.

Rude, she thought as she followed him. He was rude as well as being opinionated and arrogant, but no way was she going to allow him to continually get the better of her. It was time somebody brought him down to size. Well past time.

'I can give you half an hour, tops, because I have an admin meeting at six o'clock,' she said when they reached her office. 'If you need longer I'll come down to your office on my day off.'

'Fair enough.' He pulled a chair over to her desk, extracted a notebook from his jacket pocket, and flipped it open. 'OK, before I give you the transcript I need to confirm your personal details against those we have on file.'

'You have a file on me?' she said faintly, and he smiled without warmth.

'We have a file on everybody, Dr Kennedy. Your full name is Kate Elizabeth Kennedy. You'll be thirty-five on the 2nd of next month, your address is 33 Union Grove, and you're married to John Elliot.'

'No.'

A frown pleated his forehead. 'No, to what?'

'Your information is wrong on two counts,' she replied. 'My address is 33A Union Grove. The house is split into two, and I have the ground floor flat.'

'And the second error?'

'I…I'm not married any more,' she said, trying to sound offhand, casual, but failing miserably. 'My divorce came through on Saturday.'

'I'm sorry,' he declared, and there was genuine sympathy in his face. 'It's tough when a marriage ends acrimoniously.'

Hurt struggled with honesty within her, and honesty won.

'It wasn't an acrimonious divorce,' she said with an effort. 'He didn't leave me for somebody else. He has somebody else now, but that wasn't why he left. He left because…because he just didn't love me any more.'

Probably because he hardly ever saw me, she thought miserably, and when we did meet we seemed to have run out of things to say. Unless it was to hurl angry, hurtful words at one another.

'He was stupid.'

'I— W-what?' she stammered.

'Kate, you're bright, funny, attractive.' He shrugged. 'What else did he want?'

'He didn't…I didn't…I mean…' To her annoyance she could

feel herself blushing. *Pull yourself together, Kate. OK, so this attractive—very attractive—man has said you're bright, and funny, and attractive, but that's no reason for you to completely fall apart.* 'I…umm… Thank you.'

'Don't mention it,' he said.

Dio, but he shouldn't have either, he realised, as he saw a blush creep across her cheeks. OK, so she *was* bright, and funny and attractive, and he did think her husband was an idiot, but what the hell was he doing here? He never paid women compliments unless he was making a play for them, and he had no intention of making a play for Kate Kennedy. In fact, he'd been more than a little relieved to discover when he got back to his office on Saturday night that she was married which meant she was strictly off limits as far as he was concerned.

She still is, he told himself, as her large grey eyes met his then skittered away quickly. Divorced—separated—single—it made no difference. No way was he ever going to get involved with this woman. OK, so maybe she possessed the kind of lush, full breasts guaranteed to send a man's blood rushing to his head, and a pair of hips that simply cried out to be touched, but she was trouble. He didn't know how she possibly could be, but he could feel it, sense it.

'What can you tell me about Terri Campbell?' he said brusquely.

'What's that got to do with anything?' she asked in confusion, and saw his eyebrows snap down. 'OK— All right—for some reason best known only to yourself you want to know about Terri,' she continued quickly. 'She's worked at the General for more than twenty years, has been a sister in A and E for the past ten years, is married to Frank, and has two children—Neil and Lissa.'

'Has she any money or family worries?'

Kate blinked. Quite what he was trying to get at here was beyond her, but she had no intention of telling him anything about Terri's problems with her son, Neil. That was the sister's private business.

'None as far as I know,' she said.

'You're sure?'

'Don't you trust anybody?' she exclaimed, and his lips curled as he wrote something down in his notebook.

'God perhaps, but everyone else I regard as a suspect.'

'Wow, but with that sort of attitude you must have a real fun social life,' she said without thinking, then winced as she waited for him to explode, but to her amazement his mouth twitched into a reluctant smile.

'You're right, I don't,' he murmured. 'What can you tell me about Paul Simpson, your specialist registrar?'

'Paul?' she echoed, desperately trying to marshal her thoughts, and not think about why a man with looks like Mario Volante should have a lousy social life. 'Not a lot, really. He's worked in the department for almost a year. He's bright, efficient, and very organised.'

'And you don't like him,' he said shrewdly.

She didn't, and it had nothing to do with Paul's capabilities. He *was* bright and efficient, but she also had the distinct impression that he didn't like working for a woman. It wasn't because of anything he'd said—he was far too astute to leave himself open to an accusation of sexual bias—but there had been the occasional look, the odd throwaway comment, that had more than ruffled her.

'I can't like everybody,' she declared, suddenly realising Mario was expecting her to reply, 'and as long as he continues to work efficiently I'll have no complaints.'

'Colin Watson?'

She shook her head. 'I don't know him well enough to comment. He just qualified last month, and this is his first week with us.'

'Ah.' He smiled. 'The dreaded August intake. Never be ill or have an accident in August because that's when all the still-wet-behind-the-ears newly qualified doctors are let loose on the wards.'

'Exactly.' She could not help but laugh. 'And before you ask me about the nursing staff,' she continued, seeing him glance down at his notebook. 'As far as I'm concerned, they're all terrific, and if you want personal details about them you'll have to ask Terri. The only other member of staff I know well is our porter, Bill, who's worked in the department for twelve years, and is an absolute gem.'

Mario closed his notebook, and extracted a sheet of paper from his pocket.

'This should be an exact transcript of what you told me on Saturday night. Could you read through it, then sign it if you agree that it's accurate?'

She took the piece of paper from him, scanned it quickly, then reached for her pen.

'What about the photographs you wanted me to look at?' she said, scrawling her signature across the bottom of the page.

From his other pocket he pulled out a plastic envelope but before he could shake its contents out onto her desk, they both heard a distant thud.

Kate half rose to her feet, then slowly sat down again. If anything major had happened in the treatment room, Terri, or somebody else, would come for her. She knew that. She was fully aware of that, but the thud had sounded as though something or someone had fallen over. Maybe she ought to check it out, but Paul was on duty, and despite the fact that she didn't like him, he wasn't an idiot. Having said which…

'Your department isn't going to collapse simply because you've taken a half hour break,' Mario declared, watching her, and she flushed.

'I know.'

'It's just you don't think anybody else can do the job as well as you can,' he observed. 'So which are you—a control freak, or an over-compensator?'

John had asked her that once, too, she remembered with a stab of pain. She'd yelled back at him that nobody ever questioned a man's dedication to his work, and he had stared back at her for a long, silent moment, and then he'd walked away.

'Kate?'

Mario's eyes were fixed on her, curious, thoughtful, and she sat up straighter.

'I thought you wanted me to look at some photographs?' she declared.

For a moment she thought he was going to press the subject but, to her relief, he shook the photographs out of their packet onto her desk, then sat back.

'Take your time. Don't rush at it, but examine each one carefully.'

She was sorely tempted to tell him she wasn't an idiot, but didn't. Instead, she did as he asked, but when she'd reached the last one she shook her head.

'I'm sorry. Nobody looks even remotely familiar. As I said before—'

'You don't run out into the waiting room and stare at the people sitting there,' he finished for her. 'Don't worry about it. It was a long shot anyway, and thanks for trying.'

'Is that everything?' she asked.

'Almost.' He gathered up the photographs and pocketed them. 'You might be interested to know we've got a full ID on Duncan Hamilton. He was originally from London, and had been doing casual work around Aberdeen for the past ten months. According to his widowed mother, he was a Grade A student who dropped out of university and had never been in trouble before.'

'Then how in the world did he ever get mixed up in something like this?' Kate said, and Mario's face grew grim.

'As I told you on Saturday, it can happen to anybody. The fixers prey on the weak and the unhappy. People who are in debt, people who think they'll only have to be a mule or a body-packer once, and then all their worries will be over.'

But it was such a waste of a life, she thought, as she remembered Duncan Hamilton's face as he'd thrashed and gasped in agony on the trolley. He ought to have had his whole life ahead of him, and now his body was lying, cold and stiff, on a mortuary slab.

And then something else occurred to her.

'Your department knew Duncan was a body-packer, didn't they?' she said slowly. 'I mean, if somebody collapsed in front of me, my first thought—even though I'm a doctor—wouldn't be "body-packer", and yet the security guards at the airport immediately thought that. They were expecting him, weren't they?'

A glimmer of a smile curved his lips. 'My department could do with people like you.'

'And that is not an answer,' she pointed out, and he sighed.

'Yes, we had a tip-off about him. It happens sometimes. Just last week we picked up a girl from Colombia who turned out to have two kilograms of snow stuffed down her bra.'

'Snow?' she repeated, and he nodded.

'"Snow", "Charlie", "coke", "nose-candy"—cocaine goes by as many names as it does uses. You can snort it, smoke it, inject it, or mix it with heroin. I understand that rubbing it onto somebody's genitalia and then licking it off is considered very stimulating. Not that I've ever tried it myself, of course,' he added.

'Right,' she said, all too aware that a tide of heat was creeping up the back of her neck, and irritated beyond measure that it was.

Good grief, she was a doctor. She'd probably seen more female—and male—genitalia in her time than this man had eaten hot dinners, so what he was saying shouldn't be making her blush, but it was.

'Who tipped you off about Duncan?' she asked, deliberately changing the subject.

'His fixer.'

'His *fixer?*' she repeated. 'But, why would the man who recruits the body-packers tip you off about one of his own?'

'Because the fixer knows we can't search every passenger who comes off a plane,' Mario replied, 'so sometimes he'll phone us anonymously and give us a name. We arrest that mule or body-packer and somebody else on the plane, somebody who's carrying perhaps twenty-five times the amount of cocaine of the person we've been tipped off about, walks free.'

'So Duncan Hamilton could simply have been nothing more than an unwitting decoy?' she said in disgust, and Mario smiled, a small bitter smile.

'It's a dirty business, Kate, but it's also a very lucrative one. £6.6 billion is spent on drugs in Britain alone every year. There's a huge demand for it, and the farmers in the poorer countries of the world are only too keen to supply that market.'

'But why can't they grow something else?' she protested. 'Why can't they grow something that will help the world's population, not destroy it?'

The bitter smile on Mario's face faded to be replaced by a gentler one.

'Kate, if you were a dirt-poor farmer in Colombia, and coffee was selling on the world market for 35p a kilo while cocaine was fetching £2,000, what would you be growing? And £2,000 a kilo is peanuts compared to the mark-up. By the time that kilo has reached the UK it has a street value of around £35,000.'

'Then you're saying it isn't ever going to change!' she exclaimed. 'That there's nothing you can do that will stem the tide.'

'No, I'm not saying that. The things I've seen, Kate... Kids as young as twelve acting as body-packers, pregnant women...' His face became suddenly strained. 'I have to believe I can somehow—even in a small way—stop the death and destruction that these drugs cause. If I didn't believe it, I couldn't do my job.'

And he did it well, she knew he did. She could see the

complete commitment in his deep blue eyes. It was a commitment she understood, a commitment she shared towards her own profession, and she wondered if he'd had to pay a price for that dedication. She'd had to. Her dedication had cost her the love of a man who had once pledged to spend the rest of his life with her. Had Mario Volante needed to pay a similar price?

'Mario…' She came to a halt as the door of her office opened, and Terri's head appeared. 'Problem?' she asked, and the sister shook her head.

'I just wanted to tell you—in case you were concerned by the thud earlier—that it was nothing to worry about. Colin had a crasher in cubicle 6.'

'Thanks, Terri,' Kate replied and the sister's head disappeared again, but not before she had glanced from Mario to Kate, then back again, with patent curiosity.

'It's amazing how often it's not the patient who faints,' Mario observed once they were alone again, 'but the person who brought them in.'

'How do you know that a crasher is somebody who's fainted?' Kate asked curiously. 'Come to think of it,' she added. 'How do you know about August being the worst time to come into hospital if you're a patient?'

'Because I originally qualified as a doctor, but I found the hours a real killer.'

'Yeah, right,' she said, not bothering to hide her disbelief, 'and a policeman works nine to five, with every weekend off. Why did you give it up?'

He raked his fingers through his too-long black hair, and smiled a little ruefully.

'It was a mistake for me to go into medicine in the first place. My parents were both doctors, you see, and though they didn't pressurise me into following in their footsteps I suppose I just sort of assumed I would. I became an A and E doctor—was eventually promoted to specialist registrar—but when I hit thirty…' He shook his head. 'I realised it wasn't for me.'

'But why?' she asked, bewildered.

'I'd spent six years treating car crash victims, victims of domestic abuse, neglected children, people completely spaced out on drugs, and I thought…' He frowned, as though groping for the right words. 'Setting broken bones, patching up injuries… I wanted to stop the broken bones from happening, nail the idiots who drove at 100 miles per hour in a 40 mile zone, collar the drug pushers who offered hits for fifty pence a time to ensnare the unwary, the unhappy, the desperate.'

'You wanted to make the streets a safer place for all of us.' She smiled, and abruptly he got to his feet.

'Something like that,' he muttered. 'And now I must go. I've taken up more than enough of your time.'

He had, but now that he was going, she didn't want him to leave. She wanted to ask him why he'd chosen the drugs squad rather than any of the other police specialisations, to persuade him to tell her more about himself, and that, she thought wryly, was more than enough reason to push him out the door.

'Will I have to appear in court?' she asked as she followed him out of her office and down the corridor. 'I mean, if you catch Duncan Hamilton's fixer, will I be needed as a witness?'

'I doubt it,' he said, but he didn't meet her gaze.

Which was odd, she realised, because she was normally all too aware of his blue eyes burning into her.

'Mario—'

'*There* you are, Kate!' Paul exclaimed, coming out of the treatment room clutching a clipboard. 'Terri said you were talking to an old friend…' The specialist registrar's eyes took in Mario's creased leather jacket, faded denims and beat-up trainers, and his lip curled slightly. 'So I thought I'd better remind you—in case you'd forgotten—that you're due at an M and M meeting in fifteen minutes.'

Of course she hadn't forgotten, she thought acidly. She wished she could. Morbidity and mortality conferences were a necessary evil after a patient died, but all too often the conferences became an occasion to embarrass the consultant in charge, and she was all too aware that there were more than enough people at the General longing to see her fall flat on her face.

'That was very thoughtful of you, Paul,' she replied as evenly as she could. 'Is everything OK in the treatment room?'

'Naturally,' he said airily. 'We had a gomer in cubicle 2 earlier but I turfed him.'

A gomer. A and E shorthand for Get Out of My Emergency Room. A derogatory term applied to a geriatric patient who had multiple complicated medical problems rather than one acute one. Kate had never liked the term, and she liked it even less today.

'Don't forget you'll be old yourself one day, Paul,' she said, and saw the specialist registrar's lips clamp down hard on the retort she sensed he was itching to make.

'I see what you mean,' Mario observed as Paul hurried away in answer to his bleeper. 'I don't like him, either.'

Professional courtesy told her she should immediately spring to her specialist registrar's defence, but she was all out of courtesy today.

'He's a complete prat,' she said, and Mario laughed.

'Good luck with the D and D.' His smile widened as he saw her confusion. 'In my med days, M and M conferences were also known as death and doughnut affairs if they laid on refreshments.'

She let out a gurgle of laughter. 'I must remember that.'

'See that you do, and don't let the top brass grind you down.' He held out his hand. 'I might see you again, Kate Kennedy, and I might not. If I don't, it's been nice meeting you.'

It had certainly been different, she thought, as she shook his hand then dropped it quickly when she felt a warm tingle of sensation race up her arm, but it was better if she never saw him

again. Her work was exhausting enough without added complications, and if Mario Volante was married then he was strictly
off limits as far as she was concerned.

And if he's single? her mind whispered as she watched
him walk away.

He was still most definitely off limits, she told herself firmly.

'Have those bozos in Admin ever *tried* to save the life of a body-
packer?' Terri asked, incensed, when Kate returned from her
conference, stressed out and exhausted. 'Do they have *any* idea
of the complications, the difficulties—'

'They play it as they see it, Terri,' Kate interrupted wearily,
'so let's just forget it, OK?'

And the sister said no more, but throughout the rest of their
long and tiring shift Kate heard her muttering under her breath.

She wanted to mutter, too, but she knew it wouldn't do any
good. Duncan Hamilton had died whilst under her care and,
though nobody in Admin had come right out and said it, she knew
there was always going to be the underlying implication that he
might have lived if somebody else had been treating him.

'Would you like a lift home?' Terri asked when their shift
finally ended.

'Thanks, but I'd prefer to walk,' Kate replied. 'It might
clear my head.'

'You're sure?' Terri said uncertainly, and Kate forced a chirpy
smile to her face.

'Of course I'm sure. It's a lovely evening, and I could do with
some fresh air.'

She could, too, Kate thought, as she hitched her shoulder bag
onto her shoulder, and left the hospital. It had been a long day,
and an extremely tiring one. The kind of day when she wondered
if it was worth it. The endless paperwork, the drunken abusive
patients who almost never died, whereas the nice people, the

kind people, all too often did. And then she remembered the little girl she had treated this afternoon. Her mother had been so certain her daughter had meningitis, and the look of relief and gratitude on her face when Kate had been able to tell her that the rash was simply an allergy had been worth more than winning the lottery.

It *was* all worth it, she decided, breathing in deeply and savouring the late evening sunshine as she stepped off the pavement to get past the scaffolding that had been erected round the Edwardian building on the corner of the street. Everyone had days when they wondered whether they'd made the correct career choice. Everyone had moments when they wondered whether this was all there was to life. OK, so maybe today she'd had a bad day, but every job had its bad days.

Though maybe not quite as unremittingly awful as this one was turning out to be, she thought, as she felt someone's hands slam into her back and the next thing she knew she was lying face down in the road.

Mugger, was her first thought, but, as she turned, ready to hit out with her feet and fists at her assailant, she saw to her amazement that Mario Volante was kneeling on the ground behind her, covered in dust, and the shattered remnants of a baluster were lying in the road not six feet from where she'd been standing.

'Are you all right?' he said, getting to his feet quickly. 'Did any of that masonry hit you?'

'I'm fine,' she gasped. 'Bit winded, that's all.' She squinted up at the building from which the baluster had fallen. 'No wonder they've got all that scaffolding up. That place is literally falling to bits.'

'Kate—'

'Oh, hell, would you look at my skirt?' she continued in dismay as she got unsteadily to her feet. 'I'll never be able to mend it, and I only bought it six—'

'Forget about your skirt,' he interrupted. 'Did you notice anybody hanging about before the baluster fell?'

'Did I notice…?' Her mouth fell open. 'You think somebody deliberately pushed that baluster, don't you? Oh, for heaven's sake, Mario. The building is simply unsafe, and I was unlucky enough to be walking past it when a bit fell off.'

'Maybe.'

'Are all policemen this suspicious?' she demanded. 'Or are you just especially paranoid?'

'Kate—'

'And what are you doing here, anyway?' she continued, her eyes suddenly narrowing. 'Are you *following* me?'

'Of course I'm not following you!' he exclaimed. 'I just happened to be conducting an enquiry across the street, and came out of the house as the baluster began to fall. Come on, my car's over there. I'll drive you home.'

He had already caught hold of her arm, clearly taking her agreement for granted, and she shook herself free with annoyance.

'I don't need—or want—you to drive me home,' she replied. 'My flat's just three blocks away, and I'm perfectly capable of walking there.'

'I'm sure you are but Union Grove is not three blocks away, and I'm driving you home.'

'Don't you ever take no for an answer?' she protested, irritated beyond measure by his implacable expression. 'I am fine—OK?—and I want to walk home, so why don't you just go away and get on with your police work?'

'Because I'm fresh out of little old ladies to harass and now I'm targeting a younger age group. Kate, are you going to come quietly,' he continued, as she glared up at him, 'or am I going to have to cuff you?'

Would he? She couldn't be one hundred per cent certain that he wouldn't, and with ill-disguised bad grace, she hitched her

shoulder bag back up onto her shoulder and strode across the road
to the dusty, nondescript Volkswagen that was sitting there.

'This is ridiculous,' she said, yanking open the passenger door
and clambering in. 'Haven't you got a wife, or significant other,
to go home to?'

'My wife divorced me four years ago, and there is no significant other in my life.'

'I…I'm sorry,' she said awkwardly, 'about your wife, I mean.'

'I loved my work, my wife didn't,' he replied as he slid into
the driver's seat beside her. 'End of story. Want to talk about why
your marriage failed?'

'No.'

'Fair enough,' he replied. 'He's a doctor at the General, isn't
he, but his speciality is Orthopaedics rather than A and E.'

'How did you…? Oh, of course,' she continued tightly. 'You
have all my information on file, don't you, right down to the size
of shoes I take, and the make of my underwear.'

'We only carry detailed dossiers of known and suspected drug
dealers,' he observed, then his eyes glinted. 'But if you'd like to tell
me the make of your underwear—purely for our file, of course…'

'No, I wouldn't,' she said stonily, 'and John doesn't work at
the General any more. He got another job six months ago, and
can we drop this subject, please?'

'It must be tough when two consultants get married,' he
observed as though she hadn't spoken. 'Two huge workloads,
two equally large amounts of responsibility.'

'John isn't a consultant. He's a specialist registrar.'

'Ah.'

'And what's that supposed to mean?' she demanded.

'Some men have problems with a woman—even if that
woman is their wife—making it to the top if they haven't.'

'John isn't—wasn't—that petty,' she protested, and saw one
of Mario's eyebrows rise.

'If you say so,' he murmured.

'Look, are you driving me home any time soon?' she exclaimed. 'Or are we just going to sit in your car while you sound off about something you know nothing about?'

He shot her a sidelong glance, looked for a moment as though he was about to say something, then put the car into gear and drove off.

John hadn't been that petty, Kate told herself, as she sat in angry silence while Mario negotiated the city streets towards her home. He'd been thrilled to bits when she'd been made consultant, had even laughed when his colleagues had made jokes about who wore the trousers in their relationship.

Except, increasingly, he hadn't laughed, she remembered, hadn't said anything very much at all. *Had* her promotion bothered him? But he'd always known it was her goal. He had married her knowing she wanted to become a consultant so it couldn't have bothered him. It couldn't.

'This is where you live?' Mario said, his voice showing his clear surprise, when he drew his car to a halt outside the faded façade of number 33A, Union Grove. 'I mean, I'm sure it's very nice,' he added hurriedly, 'but I pictured you living somewhere…bigger.'

'Grander, you mean,' she said dryly. 'John and I used to have a house in Murray Terrace, but we sold it after we separated, and it didn't take me long to discover that even half of the proceeds of a house in Murray Terrace doesn't buy you very much in Aberdeen nowadays.'

'So it seems,' Mario murmured, but, when Kate put out her hand to open the car door, he stretched out his own hand to stay her. 'You know, the more I think about that baluster this evening, the more I don't like it.'

'It was *an accident*, Mario!' she exclaimed and he shook his head.

'It's too much of a coincidence—you treating Hamilton on

Saturday night, and now this. I want you to take time off work, stay home where you'll be safe.'

'In your dreams.'

'I mean it, Kate,' he insisted. 'A and E is too open, too exposed. You're surrounded by knives, and scalpels, and the security system there is lousy. You'd be dead before you hit the panic button.'

'Well, thanks for sharing that with me,' she replied. 'Mario, I can't and won't take time off. We're short-staffed enough as it is without me staying home for no good reason.'

'I've just given you a reason!' he exclaimed, and she threw him a you-must-be-kidding glance.

'All you've done is come up with some harebrained, completely illogical notion that somebody might want to kill me,' she declared, 'based, presumably, on the fact that I was one of the last people to see Hamilton alive. Why on earth would anybody want to kill me because of that?'

He opened his mouth, then closed it again.

'I still want you to take time off work.'

'No,' she replied. 'Capital N, capital O. And if you're thinking of trying any more of that Italian macho blustering on me,' she continued, seeing his brow furrow, 'you can forget it. The answer is still no.'

'OK, if you won't take time off work, I'm coming into work with you.'

She stared at him incredulously for a second, then rounded on him.

'No—absolutely not. You'll get in the way, get under everybody's feet. And I thought nobody was supposed to know you are a policeman?' she continued as he tried to interrupt. 'You're hardly going to be invisible if you're stuck to me like glue, are you?'

'I won't get in your way,' he replied. 'In fact, I might even be able to help you. I was a doctor, remember?'

'A doctor who stopped practising eight years ago,' she pointed out. 'You're probably not even on the register now.'

'Kate, I'm not stupid. I won't attempt to do a cricothyroidotomy or a thoracotomy. I'll just do the simple stuff—the cut fingers, the broken arms.'

'But—'

'OK, if you're not keen on that,' he continued, 'how about if we tell your colleagues I'm a nurse? I've been overseas for years, and I'll be in the department for a few weeks to refresh my skills. Actually, that would work better,' he added thoughtfully, 'because as a nurse I could assist you, be at your side constantly.'

Be at her side constantly? As in eight hours a day, five—and sometimes six—days a week?

'Mario, being an A and E nurse isn't some sort of soft option alternative to being a doctor!' she exclaimed. 'It requires specialised skills—'

'I know—'

'You *don't*,' she interrupted angrily. 'You were a doctor, a *male* doctor. I doubt if you even noticed what the A and E nurses were doing when you were working, far less how good they were. No way can you waltz in, and work alongside them, without them shouting, "Fake."'

'I'll talk to your bosses,' he observed, completely ignoring her, 'see if they'll permit it.'

'Don't you ever *listen?*' she protested. 'Mario—'

'Kate, could you humour me on this, please?' he said. 'Let me come into work with you.'

He wasn't threatening to handcuff her, or using his police powers to make her stay home. He was simply asking her. Asking her with his blue eyes fixed on her, full of concern, and it was that more than anything else which made her eventually sigh and nod.

'OK—all right. But only if Admin agrees to your presence,' she added quickly, seeing the triumph in his face, 'and only if you accept that if you get in the way, interfere with the smooth running of my department, I'll have the hospital security guards throw you out faster than you can say enema.'

'It's a deal,' he said, but when she got out of the car he leant over the passenger seat and grinned up at her. 'Kate, I promise you won't even know I'm there.'

He had to be kidding, she thought, as she watched him drive away. She'd be all too well aware that he was there. All too aware that this annoying, interfering, oh-so-strange attractive mixture of a man was there, but she was going to have to get used to it.

At least in the short term, she told herself, as she turned and strode up the dusty path towards her front door.

CHAPTER THREE

'OH, VERY nice, very cute,' Ralph observed, his eyes brimming with laughter as they took in Mario's white nurse's top and matching trousers. 'Want to take my pulse, Nurse Volante?'

'Want a one-way ticket to Men's Surgical, Detective Sergeant Evanton?' Mario said, closing the door of Kate's office with slightly more force than was strictly necessary. 'Nursing is a profession, Ralph, not a gender.'

'And I bet you thought that when you were a doctor, didn't you?' his detective sergeant declared, and Mario's lips twisted ruefully.

'OK, all right, I didn't,' he admitted, 'but these last three days at the General have been a steep learning curve.'

They had been, too, he thought. He had not been best pleased when the administrative department of the General had only agreed to his presence in A and E as a nursing auxiliary. He had been even less pleased to discover that the vast majority of the public and staff at the General seemed to assume he must be gay if he was a male nurse, but what had really got under his skin was when Kate had taken him aside on his first morning.

'I have only one thing to say to you,' she'd said. 'If you screw up at any point, admit it. At least then, if it's possible to be corrected, it will be corrected right away. We're all human, we all make mistakes, but don't try to hide them, OK?'

He'd been furious. *Dio*, he'd been livid. He was a fully quali-fied doctor, for heaven's sake, even if he had stopped practising eight years ago, but he'd very quickly learned that not only was eight years a long time in the medical world, but the A and E nurses were a breed apart. They possessed an inbuilt instinct and a breadth of knowledge he could only marvel at, and as for Kate… He'd worked with a lot of consultants when he was a doctor, but he'd never worked with somebody who was quite as dedicated, or quite so good.

'OK, Ralph, what have you got for me?' he asked, pulling a chair over to Kate's desk. 'And make it fast. Kate says she's the only one who uses her office but I don't want to risk anyone walking in on us.'

'So, it's Kate now, is it?'

'Ralph…'

'OK—OK,' his detective sergeant said, flipping open his notebook. 'I have some good news and some bad news. The good news is we've got a lead on Hamilton's cutter, and the forensic boys are 99.9 per cent certain that the baluster fell accidentally.'

'And the bad news?'

'We raided the addresses Kate gave us, and found nothing, which means either she got the addresses wrong, or—'

'Somebody knows Hamilton talked, and they've shut those operations down,' Mario said grimly. 'Which means the baluster probably didn't fall accidentally.'

'Mario, forensics found no signs of any chisel marks on the stonework,' Ralph protested, 'or any other sign that force might have been used to dislodge it.'

'So why aren't they 100 per cent certain it wasn't pushed?'

'Because,' Ralph said with exaggerated patience, 'there's an outside, million to one chance, that it might—just might—have been given a nudge to help it on its way.'

'Exactly.'

'Mario, a million to one chance is as good as saying it didn't happen!' Ralph exclaimed, seeing his boss's face set into tight lines. 'Look, you were following her on Monday. Did you see anything suspicious?'

'No, but—'

'And it's been five days now since Hamilton died,' the detective sergeant continued. 'OK, so the agents have moved their operations elsewhere but if they'd wanted Kate dead, they would have got her by now.'

'Maybe, but—' Mario thrust his fingers through his black hair, making it look even more untidy than usual. 'It just doesn't feel right, Ralph. Kate knows so much, and for nobody to have made a move… I can't help but feel they're simply waiting for the right opportunity.'

'This feeling,' Ralph observed, his eyes glinting. 'It couldn't possibly be clouded by the fact that our lady doctor's kind of cute?'

Cute wouldn't have been a word he would ever have used to describe Kate Kennedy, Mario thought wryly. Bloody-minded, opinionated, determined—those were the words which immediately sprang into his mind—but not cute.

'Ralph, will you quit with the matchmaking,' he declared, suddenly realising his detective sergeant was gazing slyly at him. 'I don't have time for a relationship.'

'Too right you don't if all you do is work, eat and sleep. Correction,' Ralph added. 'You don't always remember to eat and sleep.'

'You're beginning to sound more and more like my mother,' Mario declared, but Ralph refused to be sidetracked.

'Mario, I know how dedicated you are,' he said. 'Lord knows, I should after working with you for eight years, but this case…' He cleared his throat awkwardly. 'I know Kate has the same hair colouring, but she's not—'

'Enough, Ralph,' Mario interrupted, his voice clipped, tight.

'All I'm saying is,' Ralph said quickly, 'if the reason you're giving two hundred per cent to this case is because—'

'*Basta*, Ralph!' Mario exclaimed, his face brooking no opposition. 'I am here purely and simply because Kate Kennedy is the only witness we have in this case.'

Except that wasn't true, Mario realised, as he walked back into the treatment room in time to see Kate emerging from one of the cubicles with a wide smile on her face. A smile he found himself answering despite all his best efforts not to. A smile that was infectious, and warming, and reminded him so much of another woman's smile, and he didn't want to be reminded of that woman. Not now, not ever.

'Something wrong?' Kate asked, her smile faltering as she came towards him. 'Did…?' She glanced over her shoulder to make sure nobody was within earshot. 'Did your sergeant bring bad news?'

'Actually, he brought good news,' Mario replied with an effort. 'We've got a lead on Hamilton's cutter.'

'What's a cutter?' she said, clearly none the wiser.

'Cutters are the men who repackage the cocaine into small quantities so it can get through customs. Drugs were originally simply packed into condoms or balloons, you see,' he explained, seeing her continued confusion, 'and the body-packer simply swallowed them. Now, because of improved X-ray facilities at airports, the cutters need to know how to alter the radio density of the packages.'

'And they can do that?' she said in amazement, and he nodded.

'One of the favourite ways is to cover the condom or balloon with several layers of latex, then seal it with a hard wax coating to which you've added aluminium foil, plastic food wrap, even carbon paper.'

She shuddered. 'Just the thought of swallowing a mixture like that is enough to make me want to throw up.'

'Me, too,' he said, 'but, sadly, there's enough people prepared to do it.'

'But…' She frowned slightly. 'How is having a lead on Duncan Hamilton's cutter going to help you?'

'Because the cutters work to order,' he replied. 'The fixer contacts the cutter to tell him what he wants. If we get the cutter, we'll hopefully be able to persuade him to tell us who his fixer is, and that will take us one step closer to Mr Big himself.'

'I see,' she said, and he saw hope stir in her eyes. 'Having this lead on Hamilton's cutter… Does that mean you won't have to keep on working here?'

'Want rid of me already?' he said, then cursed himself inwardly when a faint tinge of colour darkened her cheeks.

In nome di Dio, but *why* did he keep on trying to flirt with her? It wasn't as though she was even his type. His type were tall, leggy, placid brunettes, not rounded little auburn-haired women with attitude. OK, so her hair was beautiful, and she possessed a pair of the loveliest grey eyes he'd ever seen, plus a cleavage guaranteed to give any red blooded male a headache, but she was also argumentative and opinionated, and no way did he ever want to get involved with somebody like that. She'd drive him crazy in a month.

'Kate—'

'Too right, I want rid of you,' she said tartly. 'You're too damned disruptive. If our female patients aren't making eyes at you, our male ones are propositioning you.'

And that was why he kept flirting with her, he thought, as he burst out laughing. Because she never let him get away with it. Because though she might blush, and be initially flustered, she always came back at him, and he'd never met another woman who could do that. Not even the woman whose memories he kept locked in a box labelled *Do not open*.

'Kate, listen—'

'Can I expect you in cubicle 5 any time this evening, Nurse Volante?' Paul Simpson declared, appearing without warning beside them. 'Or are you simply with us as an ornament?'

'Sorry, Doctor,' Mario replied meekly, but he exhaled through his teeth when Paul walked away, and Kate gazed at him sympathetically.

'I'm afraid Paul has a rather unfortunate manner with the nurses,' she began. 'He's a good doctor—'

'He is also a jerk,' Mario interrupted, and Kate's lips twitched.

'He certainly doesn't seem to like you very much,' she conceded, then her smile deepened. 'Maybe he's afraid you're going to ask him out.'

'Tell him he can sleep easy. I prefer the more macho type,' Mario replied and, as he crossed the treatment room, Kate had to bite down hard on her lip to stop herself from laughing.

He was impossible—absolutely impossible—but she couldn't help but like him. More than like him, if she was honest, but she was very proud of the way she was managing to keep a lid on her feelings, and whenever the lid threatened to blow off he invariably said something which riled her, which was fine.

Sort of.

'He's fitting in really well, isn't he?' Terri observed, seeing the direction of Kate's gaze as she joined her. 'And, boy, does he suit that uniform. I thought he was a good-looking man when he was wearing those denims and had all that stubble, but clean-shaven, and dressed in a nurse's whites...' She smacked her lips. 'Definite eye candy.'

'For both sexes, it would appear.' Kate laughed, and Terri did, too.

'I don't know why so many of our male patients assume he must be gay,' the sister observed. 'I suppose it's stereotyping—the supposition that if you're a nurse you must be a woman—but if ever there was a male man, Mario Volante is it.'

He was, too, Kate thought. Very male. Extremely male. Toe-curlingly, every-nerve-ending-aware male.

And you're only just divorced, her mind reminded her. You're off men for the duration, remember? And she was. She most definitely was, but if she was ever to fall off the wagon…

No, absolutely not, she told herself. She'd need her head examined if she was ever to get involved with a man like Mario Volante. Always presupposing he wanted to get involved with her, she thought with a slight sigh, and she wasn't at all certain that he did. For sure he flirted with her, and for sure he continually teased her, but that was all he'd done. He'd never asked her out, not even for a coffee in the canteen.

'It's odd, though,' Terri continued with a slight frown, 'but I would never have pegged Mario as a nurse, far less an auxiliary nurse, and it's not just because of the breadth of his knowledge. It's his whole manner. As though he's used to giving orders, rather than taking them. Maybe it's because he's worked overseas. Maybe nurses are given more authority there than they are here?'

Oh, hell, Kate thought, as she stared at the sister. Mario's decision to come into work with her had been made so fast that they hadn't had time to concoct even the most rudimentary of back stories for him. Most of the unit nurses had settled for his vague 'I've been overseas for the past eight years' story, but Paul would persist in asking Mario about the hospitals he'd worked in, and if Terri started doing it, too…

'Terri—'

'Are you two going to move out of my way?' Bill, their porter, snapped. 'Or am I supposed to levitate this damn thing over you?'

'Sorry, Bill,' Kate said, moving quickly aside so the porter could get past them with the wheelchair he was pushing, but a small frown pleated her forehead when he grumbled his way out of the treatment room. 'What's up with him today? He's not usually so snippy.'

'He heard yesterday that one of his granddaughters in New Zealand has been in a car crash,' Terri replied, 'and he's stressed about not being able to afford to go out and see her.'

'Oh, the poor man!' Kate exclaimed. 'Is there anything we can do?'

'I was wondering whether we could perhaps organise a whip-round, or something?' Terri declared. 'We'd have to do it tactfully—you know how Bill feels about charity—but if we did it carefully, bought him the plane ticket…'

'I think that's an excellent idea,' Kate said. 'Maybe we could tell him…' She paused. Mario and Paul were standing outside cubicle 5, practically nose to nose, and she didn't think they were exchanging telephone numbers. 'What the…?'

'If I were in the business of making educated guesses,' Terri murmured, 'I'd say Paul and Mario were having a humdinger of a row.'

That would have been Kate's guess, too, and she stepped forward, only to stop. The nursing staff weren't her responsibility, they were Terri's, but the sister must have read her mind because she shook her head quickly.

'Nope—absolutely not,' she declared. 'No way am I getting in between those two.'

And before Kate could say anything Terri had slipped into one of the cubicles, leaving her with no alternative but to walk slowly and extremely reluctantly towards the two men.

'Kate, could you explain to this…this moron that I'm the specialist registrar in this department,' Paul exclaimed as soon as she drew near, 'and that when I give an order I expect it to be obeyed.'

'Even if it's wrong?' Mario retorted, and Kate groaned inwardly.

She didn't need this, she really didn't. They had a waiting room full of people, and yet every nurse in the treatment room was standing, frozen, watching to see what she would do.

'Can I have a word, Nurse Volante?' she said.

'But—'

'*Now*, Nurse Volante,' Kate continued, and waited only until they were out of Paul's earshot before she muttered, 'OK, I know Paul can sometimes be a jerk, but—'

'This has nothing to do with Paul's personality,' Mario interrupted. 'He thinks the man in cubicle 5 has viral hepatitis, and I think it's something else, so I want you to examine him.'

'You want me to...?' Kate gazed at Mario in horror. 'You know I can't. No matter what I might think of Paul, he's my specialist registrar, and I can't query his diagnosis.'

'I'm not asking you to query it,' Mario declared. 'I'm asking you to confirm it.'

'But that's the same as asking me to query it,' she protested. 'It would be completely unprofessional, Mario.'

'Please, Kate. I wouldn't ask you to do this if I didn't truly believe I am right and Paul is wrong.'

His blue eyes were fixed on hers, and she bit her lip.

'Every time you say, "please", and I agree to whatever you're suggesting, I live to regret it,' she observed, then sighed as she saw Mario open his mouth, clearly intending to continue the argument. 'OK, all right. I'll take a look at this patient, and I hope to heaven you're right.'

'I'm sorry, but I think Mr Nicolson has viral hepatitis,' Kate declared, taking her stethoscope out of her ears as she straightened up, and Paul shot Mario a look that spoke volumes.

'Well, now we've established that!' the specialist registrar exclaimed. 'Can I please get on with treating him?'

'Kate, have you seen Mr Nicolson's clothes?' Mario declared, completely ignoring Paul. 'He was wearing a hand woven jacket when he came in, and his shirt's unbleached linen.'

'While I'm sure your knowledge of fabrics is absolutely fascinating, Nurse Volante,' Paul replied, his voice positively glacial, 'I hardly think this is relevant, do you?'

'His wife said they pride themselves on growing as much of

their own food as they can,' Mario continued doggedly. 'Of being self-sufficient, living off the land.'

'Lot's of people do, Mario,' Kate said gently. 'Organic farming is really big now, and as Paul said—'

'I think Mr Nicolson has eaten something poisonous, and my guess is mushrooms.'

'Mushrooms?' Kate repeated as Paul uttered a barely disguised exclamation of impatience. 'Why mushrooms?'

'Because I've seen the symptoms before,' Mario declared. 'In my work.'

'They have epidemics of mushroom poisonings overseas, do they?' Paul said with derision, but Kate's gaze was fixed on Mario.

He hadn't meant what Paul thought, and she knew he hadn't.

'OK, run through his symptoms for me again,' she said, and though Paul's eyes rose heavenwards in exasperation there was no way the specialist registrar could refuse to answer her.

'Mr Nicolson developed severe abdominal pain, with persistent vomiting and watery diarrhoea yesterday morning,' he declared. 'He was also extremely thirsty, and yet despite all the fluid he drank he couldn't produce any urine. By last night he seemed a lot better, but this morning he could hardly get out of bed, seemed to have no energy, and the pain in his stomach was back. In other words, he has all the classic symptoms of viral hepatitis.'

But those symptoms could also fit mushroom poisoning, Kate thought, staring down at Grant Nicolson, and the longer they waited the more likelihood there was of his liver being irreparably damaged.

'Get his wife in here,' she said. 'I want to talk to her.'

'You…you're actually giving credence to the half-baked theory of an *auxiliary nurse?*' Paul said, two livid spots of colour appearing on his cheeks, as Mario sped away. 'You're actually going to overrule my considered, professional—'

'I'm not overruling anything,' Kate interrupted. 'I simply want to talk to Mrs Nicolson.'

'But…'

Paul bit off whatever he'd been about to say as Mario reappeared with Grant Nicolson's wife and Kate smiled encouragingly at the woman.

'Mrs Nicolson, has your husband eaten anything you haven't in the last seventy-two hours?'

'Definitely not,' the woman replied. 'We always eat the same things. Our own home-made muesli for breakfast, home-made soup for lunch, and—'

'He couldn't perhaps have eaten something when he was away from home?' Kate interrupted, and Mrs Nicolson shook her head.

'We both work from home, Doctor. Grant and I used to have high-powered jobs in London, but we weren't happy so we moved to Aberdeenshire three years ago and since then I've been working as a potter, and Grant has started his own smallholding. If we do make any trips, we make them together.'

'So there is nothing he can have eaten that you didn't?' Kate declared.

'Nothing at all.'

'Well, there you are,' Paul said. 'Now, if I might be allowed—'

'Unless you count the mushrooms we gathered on Tuesday afternoon,' Mrs Nicolson added. 'I didn't eat any because I don't like mushrooms, but they can't have made Grant ill. He was perfectly fine after he'd eaten them.'

He would have been, Kate thought, because it could take forty-eight hours for some of the more deadly mushrooms to have their effect.

'I don't suppose you have any of the mushrooms left?' she asked, all too certain that the answer would be no, but to her surprise Mrs Nicolson smiled.

'As a matter of fact, I do. I was going to take some round to my friend's house this morning, but when Grant became ill…' She delved into her capacious handbag, and produced a brown paper bag. 'As you can see, they're just ordinary field mushrooms.'

Not ordinary field mushrooms at all, Kate thought as she took the paper bag from Mrs Nicolson and shook the contents out onto a kidney dish, but death cap mushrooms. Death cap mushrooms that were full of deadly toxins which attacked the liver, and heart, and could also cause skeletal muscular damage.

'Is there something wrong?' Mrs Nicolson said hesitantly, her eyes going from Kate to Mario, to Paul, then back again. 'They *are* just ordinary mushrooms, aren't they?'

'I'm afraid they're not, Mrs Nicolson,' Kate replied. 'What you and your husband picked on Tuesday were death cap mushrooms.'

Mrs Nicolson clasped a hand to her mouth in horror, and when Mario quickly ushered her out of the cubicle, Kate stared awkwardly at her specialist registrar.

'Paul—'

'It's too late for us to pump out his stomach—the toxins will already be far too well dispersed through his system,' he interrupted stonily, 'so I'll try to correct his electrolyte imbalance by giving him thioctic acid, corticosteroids and high dosages of penicillin.'

'Paul—'

'I'll also send samples to the lab with a request for them to specifically look for indicators of elevated LDH, and bilirubin levels in Mr Nicolson's liver,' he continued, his face blank and expressionless, 'and notify IC that we'll be sending them a case of amanita poisoning.'

'Paul, if it's any consolation, mushroom poisoning wouldn't have been my first diagnosis either,' she said gently, but the specialist registrar either didn't hear her or didn't choose to.

'Do you think we got him in time?' Mario asked after Mr Nicolson had been transferred to IC and he and Kate were standing alone at the end of the treatment room.

'I don't know.' Kate sighed. 'Even if he recovers, it's pretty well certain he's going to be looking at a liver transplant.'

'It's a hard way for someone to learn that living off the land isn't necessarily always a healthy option,' Mario observed, and Kate nodded.

'What made you think it was mushroom poisoning?' she asked. 'I know you said you'd seen it before, but…'

Mario shrugged matter-of-factly. 'In my line of work, we mostly see people who have taken magic mushrooms—the ones which will give you a psychedelic high—but occasionally we come across the dummies who think they've eaten magic mushrooms only to discover they've eaten the deadly ones instead.'

'It's just as well you were here today,' she observed, but, when Paul strode past them without a word, Mario's eyebrows rose.

'I'd say it's also pretty well scotches any chance of me and Paul ever bonding,' he observed, and Kate's lips curved.

'Well, you did say you didn't think he was your type anyway,' she declared, and Mario laughed.

'Too true. In fact—'

'Look, I really would appreciate it if you people could find somewhere else to have your conversations,' Bill interrupted, as he struggled to manoeuvre the wheelchair he was pushing past them. 'This poor girl is supposed to be having her arm X-rayed, and she'd get there a hell of a lot faster if I didn't have to keep making a detour round people.'

'This is your absolute gem?' Mario remarked, as he and Kate stepped aside, and Bill pushed the wheelchair past them, still muttering. 'Seems more like a Mr Grumpy to me.'

'He's got a lot on his mind at the moment,' Kate replied. 'Apparently one of his granddaughters in New Zealand was in a car crash, and he's very worried about her. Which reminds me,' she continued. 'Terri wondered if we could perhaps do some sort of whip-round for him to raise the air fare. I'd better make sure she's got the ball rolling.'

Mario stared thoughtfully at her for a second, then nodded as though he'd resolved something he'd been puzzling over.

'Not a control freak,' he observed. 'An over-compensator.'

'I am *not*.'

'Kate, it takes one to know one,' he declared as she glared at him, fury plain on her face, 'and I'm not surprised. You're a woman in what is still seen largely as a man's profession, and to make it to the top you'd either need to be as tough as old boots—which you most certainly are not—or a person who obsessively dots every "I" and crosses every "T", to make sure everything's been done correctly.'

'And if I'm an over-compensator because I'm a woman, then what's your excuse?' she demanded, only partly mollified by his observation.

'I've spent the last eight years of my life in the police force trying to live down the fact that I have a degree.'

'Why on earth should you need to live it down?' she said, puzzled.

'Because if you have a degree—no matter what that degree is in—you're automatically fast-tracked which doesn't make you the most popular guy in the force.'

'But—'

'I didn't do time on the beat, Kate. I'm one of those new flash graduates who thinks he knows it all.' Mario smiled ruefully. 'Eight years on the job, and everybody's still waiting for me to fall flat on my face.'

'They're waiting for me to do that, too,' she admitted. 'I guess that's why I'm always the first one in the department, and the last one out. Why I constantly check and double-check everything.'

'Right down to whether Terri will remember to start the whip-round,' Mario said, and Kate bit her lip.

'It's pathetic, isn't it? What I do… It used to drive my ex mad.'

'That was his problem, not yours.'

'Was it?' she said uncertainly, her grey eyes clouded. 'Sometimes I wonder—'

'Don't,' he said firmly. 'Don't ever wonder. You're a first-rate doctor and a first-rate consultant, but more importantly you're a pretty nice human being, so you have nothing to apologise for.'

He thought she was a pretty nice human being.

Why should that mean so much to her? she wondered as she stared up at him and felt tears unaccountably clog her throat. Because he meant it, she realised. Because this big, tough cop, who had seen as much of the horrors of humanity as she had, hadn't picked out her medical skills as being the most important thing about her, hadn't even tried to turn the situation into an occasion to flirt with her, he had simply said she was a pretty nice human being, and he had meant it.

'You're not so bad yourself,' she said shakily, and he smiled.

A wide, warm smile that seemed to reach out and surround her, but as her own lips shyly curved in response, the smile in his eyes suddenly disappeared and in its place she saw a deep and unutterable sadness. A sadness that made no sense to her at all, and instinctively she put out her hand to him.

'Mario…?'

'Kate, you are never going to believe this!' Terri exclaimed as she hurried into the treatment room, then paused. 'Sorry, did I interrupt something?'

'No—'

'Absolutely not—'

She and Mario had spoken in unison, Kate realised, and deliberately she avoided his gaze.

'What won't I believe, Terri?' she said as evenly as she could, and the sister shook her head.

'You have to see this for yourself.'

And Kate did.

'Why does the waiting room look as though it's been taken over by the cast of a Wild West movie?' she asked faintly, as she gazed out over the sea of Stetsons, cowboy boots and denim.

'Because there's been a bit of a fracas at the Silver Dollar pub,' Terri explained. 'It was a line dancing night, and somebody made a comment about General Custer's girlfriend, and then Wyatt Earp pitched in with his dollar's worth, and Annie Oakley decided she wasn't having any, and… Well, it all got a bit out of hand.'

'So, I see,' Kate said, not knowing whether to laugh or cry at the number of people who were gazing back at her with bloody noses, black eyes and split lips. 'OK, let's get some triage working here. Where's Colin?' The junior doctor appeared from behind her, looking every bit as stunned as she felt. 'You take the broken noses and split lips. Paul—'

'There's an MVA on the way,' the specialist registrar interrupted stiffly. 'Two car pile-up on the outskirts of the city, serious chest injuries, and multiple fractures.'

'OK, Terri and Colin, you assist Paul with the MVA. Mario…' She squared her shoulders. 'You and I will clean up Dodge City.'

And they did, but it took a long time. A very long time.

'Just how many people were in this pub?' Kate asked wearily after she'd shepherded what felt like the fiftieth middle-aged man with a series of steri-strips across his nose out of the treatment room.

'Line dancing's very popular,' Mario murmured, 'as is country and western music.'

'Heaven alone knows why,' Kate exclaimed with irritation. 'All this stand-by-your-man garbage even if he grinds your face into the dust. Who on earth can ever take that seriously?'

'Hey, save your anger for your ex,' Mario protested. 'I'm just an innocent bystander here.'

'I'm not getting at my ex,' Kate declared. 'I just don't get country music. All they ever sing about is how their wives or husbands have left them, the farm has burned down, and their dogs have been run over.'

'I expect you like classical music,' he declared. 'Opera, that sort of thing.'

She did, but something about the way he said it had her bristling instantly.

'Actually, I'm more of a heavy metal rock fan,' she said, and he gave her a long, sideways glance.

'Uh-huh.'

'Why shouldn't I be?' she protested, but his silence was so deafening that she added quickly, 'Are there any more hillbillies out there?'

'I think that was the last one, but I'll go check.'

He strode out of the treatment room and as Kate washed her hands she noticed Colin scurrying out of cubicle 2.

'How did the MVA go?' she asked.

'One DOA, the other went up to Theatre about an hour ago.'

The junior doctor looked stressed, and exhausted, and near to tears, and Kate walked over to him.

'You OK?' she asked, and Colin tried for a smile but didn't pull it off.

'A and E… It's a lot more fraught than I'd thought it would be,' he admitted. 'I'm enjoying it, of course,' he added swiftly, 'but—'

'You wonder how you're ever going to cope,' Kate finished for him. 'Colin, we all feel that on the bad days. The days when we lose a patient, or some particularly obnoxious drunk questions our parentage. What you're feeling—it's perfectly normal.'

'Dr Simpson doesn't seem to think so,' Colin muttered, and Kate straightened up.

'Paul is not head of this department, Colin, I am, and if I say what you're feeling is normal, then it is, OK?'

The junior doctor gave her a wobbly smile, but when he went

back into cubicle 2 she saw that Mario had come back and was watching her.

'What you just said to Colin wasn't kind, and it wasn't helpful,' he observed. 'If he can't hack it now, he sure as hell isn't going to be able to when you're not around to hold his hand.'

For a second she gazed at him in stunned disbelief, then her chin came up.

'Now, listen here, Mario Volante,' she began, but he didn't let her finish.

'You need guts to survive in A and E, Kate, and if it had been me, I would have told him to get out now because he hasn't got them.'

'Well, lucky for him, I'm *not* you,' she retorted. 'Dammit, must you *always* be so cynical about everything?'

'Just telling it as I see it, Kate.'

'Then you're telling it wrong,' she declared, and Mario shrugged.

'If you say so,' he replied. 'Oh, and I was right about the hill-billies,' he added. 'That was the last one.'

And what is it with you? she wanted to say as she watched him begin to erase the name of the last country and western fan they had treated from the whiteboard. One minute you're being all kind, and supportive, and the next...

She just didn't understand him. She didn't understand him at all, and with a shake of her head she turned to see who was next on the waiting list only to notice a wallet lying on the floor of cubicle 4.

The country and western fan must have dropped it. It happened all the time. People were always leaving things behind in A and E. False teeth, walking sticks, handbags. Once Terri had even found a set of extremely sexy underwear which had them all laughing and speculating for weeks.

With a sigh she walked over to the cubicle and picked the wallet up, but as she did a photograph fell out. A photograph of a young woman with long auburn hair. A young woman who actually looked a little bit like her. Of course the girl was considerably slimmer, not to mention being much prettier, but her hair colouring was the same, and…

'That's mine.'

She looked up to see Mario standing in front of her, his face expressionless, and felt her cheeks prickle with heat.

'I—I wasn't snooping—honestly I wasn't,' she stammered. 'The photograph just fell out of the wallet when I picked it up. I didn't know it was yours.'

'No.'

Oh, hell, but she'd rather he yelled at her—even accused her of stealing—than simply stared at her with absolutely no warmth at all.

'She… She's very pretty,' she said, holding the wallet and photograph out to him. 'The girl in the photograph.'

'Yes.'

She waited for him to say that the girl was his wife, or his sister, but he didn't. He simply slid the photograph back into his wallet and pocketed it, and she forced a smile to her lips.

'I wouldn't recommend keeping your wallet in your pocket. You'd be surprised at how many light-fingered types come into A and E.'

'No, I wouldn't.'

And I want somebody—anybody—to come and interrupt us, Kate thought, as she gazed uncomfortably into his blank face. Somehow she had inadvertently intruded on something deeply personal and she wished with all her heart that she'd never seen the wallet, never picked it up, and most of all she wished she had never seen the damned photograph.

'Kate, I've got what looks like a case of food poisoning here,' Terri declared, sticking her head out of cubicle 3. 'Vomiting, diarrhoea, and her last meal was a hamburger at a friend's barbecue.'

Kate didn't care what the case was. She was just overwhelmingly relieved to have a legitimate excuse to get out of Mario's company for a few minutes, but her relief quickly turned to dismay. Within an hour, the waiting room was filled to overflowing again, and virtually each and every one of the patients had food poisoning.

'Well, at least we know what the theme of the night is,' Terri said as she helped the white-faced, middle-aged man they'd been treating out of the cubicle. 'Last night it was chest pains, tonight it's food poisoning. Funny how that often happens, isn't it?'

'Hilarious,' Kate said grimly. 'If I had my way I'd ban all barbecues.'

'Oh, come on, you can't really blame people for wanting to take advantage of this hot weather,' Terri pointed out. 'Let's face it, Aberdeen doesn't usually get the kind of weather associated with the Bahamas, so people want to enjoy it.'

'Yes, but can't they enjoy it without having a barbecue?' Kate protested. 'Or, if they're going to have one, can't they at least make sure their food is cooked thoroughly and to a high enough temperature? At this rate, we're going to run out of tetracycline.' She glanced round the treatment room, and frowned. 'Where's Mario?'

'Cubicle 6.'

Something in Terri's voice made Kate look round quickly.

'He's not having another row with Paul, is he?' she said. 'Tell me he isn't. I really don't think I—'

'The police bought in three youngsters half an hour ago,' Terri interrupted, her face grim. 'Two girls and a boy, aged between three and nine. One of the neighbours noticed the youngest one rummaging in her dustbin, and asked what she was doing. Turns out the kids have been living off breakfast cereal for the past week because mum took off on holiday to Spain with her boyfriend a fortnight ago.'

'And left them behind?' Kate said faintly.

'According to the kids, she gave them fifty pounds to feed themselves, but a teenager robbed them on their first trip to the shops.'

'Why didn't they tell somebody—this neighbour, or the police?' Kate asked with dismay, and Terri sighed.

'Because the nine-year-old is smart enough to know if she blew the whistle on mum they'd all end up in foster care, and none of them wants that.'

Kate bit her lip. No matter what she saw in her work, the sheer thoughtlessness, stupidity and utter callousness of human beings never ceased to amaze her. Maybe it would one day, but she knew that if that day ever came it would be time for her to hand in her notice.

'How's Mario coping?' she said, remembering how angry he had been earlier. 'Kids can be difficult, especially if they're traumatised.'

'He's doing brilliantly,' Terri replied. 'After Paul checked them over and pronounced them all to be a little malnourished but otherwise medically fit, Mario sent down to the kitchens for some food for them, and he's been keeping them entertained ever since.'

He still was, Kate realised, as she walked over to cubicle 6. She could hear his deep voice, and it sounded as though he was telling the children a story so she waited until he'd stopped, then poked her head round the curtains.

'Need any help?' she asked, though it was obvious he didn't from the smiles on the faces of the children.

It was also rather obvious that there was a very strong smell of dried urine and faeces emanating from the three children, but it didn't seem to bother Mario. He grinned back at her as he sat on the examination trolley, with the youngest girl on his knee, and the two older children tucked in on either side of him.

'We're doing just fine,' he said. 'In fact, you're just in time to hear my updated Cinderella story. The one where Cinders leaves her kitchen, becomes a kick-ass detective and arrests her stepsisters for speeding.'

'How come Cinders doesn't become a kick-ass consultant?' she protested, relieved to see his taut, closed expression had gone.

'Because she wouldn't get to put the baddies in jail.'

And that Mario would dearly have liked to put the mother of the three children in jail was plain from his expression when the social services arrived and the children were removed from the treatment room, tears streaming down their faces.

'What a mess.' Kate sighed as she watched the children go. 'What's going to happen to them, Mario?'

'If we can't find their mother, and the chances are we won't when all the kids know is she's somewhere in Spain,' he replied, 'they'll have to be placed in foster homes.'

'Exactly what they didn't want,' Kate murmured, and he nodded. 'You were terrific with them,' she added, trying to make him feel better. 'Do you have kids of your own?'

'My wife and I didn't have any. Just as well, really, considering we got divorced.'

'You must have younger sisters or brothers, then,' she said, remembering the girl in the photograph, and saw his face darken.

'No, I don't.'

'Maybe you're just an instinctive dad,' she said, hoping to provoke at least a smile, but she didn't get one.

'And maybe I should get back to work,' he said instead, and before she could stop him he had turned on his heel leaving her staring, bewildered, after him.

'What did I say?' she asked as Terri joined her, and the sister shrugged.

'Beats me. Maybe he just doesn't like being considered caring. You know what some men are like. They think if you tell them they're caring, what you really mean is they're soft.'

'Maybe,' Kate murmured, but she didn't believe it for a minute. A man like Mario, who could make—and take—so many jokes at the expense of his own sexuality, wouldn't have given a damn about what other people thought. Somehow her words had inadvertently hit a very raw spot inside him, and she would dearly like to know what it was.

CHAPTER FOUR

KATE sighed as she watched the elderly man and his wife walk slowly back down the treatment room. He had been so apologetic as she'd stitched the bad gash he'd sustained in his leg after he'd fallen in the street, so worried that he was taking up too much of her time and he hadn't. He had been a gentleman in every sense of the word, gently joking about his whole body starting to fall apart now he was eighty, calling her 'Miss', which nobody ever did nowadays.

'Problem?' Terri asked, pausing as she passed her, and Kate shook her head.

'I'm just thinking what a very nice couple they are.'

'People like that—they're a dying breed,' the sister observed. 'Polite, willing to wait for as long as it takes, grateful for the help we've given them… Yup, definitely a dying breed.'

They were, too. In A and E people yelled, swore and fought, and that wasn't just the psychiatric patients who had forgotten to take their medication. It was the ordinary members of the public, too. People who would never normally raise their voices, and yet the minute they came into the unit they seemed to leave any compassion and human grace they possessed at the door.

'Did I hear him say he and his wife had been married for over fifty years?' Terri continued and, when Kate nodded, she chuckled. 'Yikes, but he would have got a shorter sentence if he'd murdered her.'

Kate laughed, too, but as she watched the elderly man's wife gently help him through the door, a lump unexpectedly filled her throat.

'I picked the right man, dear,' the elderly woman had replied when Kate had asked her for the secret of her long and happy marriage, 'and I never ever let the sun go down on my anger.'

It sounded so simple, Kate thought, as she heard the distant, all too familiar sound of an approaching siren, but how did you know if you'd picked the right man? She'd thought she had when she'd married John, but she quite clearly hadn't. OK, so she had also all too frequently gone to bed angry, but surely if John had been right for her they shouldn't have had quite so many arguments in the first place?

'Two ambulances on the way,' Mario declared. 'Hit-and-run, and a motorcycle accident.' His forehead furrowed slightly. 'You all right?'

'Fine,' she said, dredging up a smile. 'Just fine.'

But she wasn't fine, she thought, as he hurried down the treatment room and she watched him go.

A week. She had only known him a week, and yet sometimes she felt as though she'd known him a lifetime. Of course, she didn't *really* know him, not properly. She knew he kept a photograph of a girl in his wallet. She knew he hated drunk drivers and couldn't bear cruelty to children. She also knew he enjoyed teasing and flirting with her but, increasingly, she'd caught him staring at her with an odd, almost hard look in his eyes. She'd tried calling him on it, demanding to know what was wrong, but he'd immediately sprung into teasing mode, leaving her wondering if she had perhaps imagined that look, but she knew she hadn't.

Does it matter if you don't understand him? she asked herself, as she heard the clatter of the outside door which meant an ambulance had arrived. Does it matter if there are huge areas of his life that you know nothing about? In a couple of weeks he'll be gone, and you'll be able to get your life back to normal. There'll be no more teasing, no more irritating wind-ups. It will be lovely and peaceful.

And dull.

'Is it the hit-and-run, or the motorcyclist?' she asked, pulling herself together as Mario appeared beside two paramedics who were pushing a trolley.

'Hit-and-run, Doc,' one of the paramedics replied. 'White married male, name Ewan Fraser, aged forty-five, compound fractures to his right and left tibia and fibula. A member of the public said he was thrown up onto the bonnet of the car, then catapulted back onto the road.'

'And the driver didn't stop?' Kate exclaimed, and the paramedic shook his head.

'Makes you wonder, doesn't it, Doc?'

It did indeed, she thought.

'GCS and BP?' she asked.

'2-2-4, 60 over 40.'

Both scores were much too low, even taking into account the fractures Ewan Fraser had sustained and the fact that his face and arms were a mess. He would eventually need the skills of both orthopaedics and plastics, but it was his laboured, rasping breathing that concerned her most.

'OK, folks, ABCs and fast,' she instructed. 'Terri, get me a BP, and pulse, then cut his clothes off. Mario—'

'I'll insert an endotracheal tube,' he finished for her, and Kate wished she was standing closer to him so she could stand on his foot as Terri shot him a startled glance.

He'd been doing that increasingly over the past week, both sounding and behaving more and more like the doctor he had been rather than the auxiliary nurse he was supposed to be, and if he wasn't careful he was going to blow his cover. She supposed she would have been the same if she had tried to masquerade as a nurse, but she was going to have to warn him about it, and the sooner the better.

'I was about to say would you take care of the IV lines, and attach him to the heart monitor while I intubate him?' she said pointedly, and for a second Mario looked bemused but—to his credit—he nodded quickly and did what she'd said.

'BP now, Terri?' Kate asked after she had gently eased the endotracheal tube past the man's vocal cords and into his trachea.

'Still 60 over 40,' the sister replied, and Kate frowned.

It should have been going up, not remaining stationary.

'IV lines?' she said.

'Open and running,' Mario replied, checking the drip bags containing the saline solution which was providing a temporary substitute for the blood the man was losing.

Quickly, Kate placed her stethoscope on the man's chest. Damn, but she could hear no breath sounds at all on the left side. Ewan Fraser's left lung must have collapsed, sending blood and air seeping into his chest cavity.

'Chest and…' She came to a halt as she realised that Mario was already holding out a chest drain and a scalpel to her. 'You know, you're going to make someone a wonderful wife,' she said lightly, and he laughed, but Terri, she noticed, didn't.

In fact, the sister was staring at Mario with a thoughtful, puzzled expression, and Kate bit her lip. She really was going to have to have a long talk with Mario, but not now. Now she needed to concentrate on making an incision into the upper right hand side of Ewan Fraser's chest, then carefully inserting a plastic tube directly into his chest cavity.

'BP now?' she asked after she'd checked with her stethoscope that the chest drain was in the right place.

'No change,' Terri replied, drawing blood out of a vein in the man's arm, and putting it into separate colour-coded vials to send off to the lab for analysis.

Damn it, but the blood pressure should be going up, not remaining static. *Why* wasn't it going up?

'OK, I want neck, chest and pelvis X-rays, and a CAT scan,' Kate declared. 'He could be bleeding inside his head, so we'd better—'

'Run the O-negative fast,' Mario declared.

He was doing it again, Kate thought, but this time she didn't have time to shoot him a warning glance. She simply nodded to Terri who swiftly inserted another IV line to take the O-negative blood they would use until they'd made a cross-match.

'I also want a chem-7,' Kate ordered. 'Low potassium can cause irregular heartbeats and—'

'No pulse, Kate!' Terri exclaimed.

For a second they all froze, then Kate raced round the examination trolley.

'OK, get me epi, and a blood gas. Mario…'

He hadn't needed any instructions. He'd already started CPR, but neither the CPR nor the blood they pumped in, two units wide open, helped. Every time Mario stopped the CPR, and they all looked at the monitor, hoping to see some kind of rhythm being established, there was none.

'Paddles, Terri,' Kate demanded.

Swiftly, the sister picked them up, and Kate gritted her teeth. This was going to be a tough one. Ewan Fraser must have weighed well over 230 lbs so she was going to have to press down really hard with her full weight to kick-start his heart. OK, so she was no size 10, but right at this moment she couldn't help but wish she was a lot heavier, and a good deal taller.

'Let me do it,' Mario said, clearly reading her mind.

If Paul had suggested such a thing he would have been lying

flat on his back, nursing a bloody nose, but as Mario gazed at her, his blue eyes steady and intent, she found herself wavering.

'You're sure?' she said uncertainly, and he nodded.

'There are some things you never forget, Kate.'

For a second she hesitated, then murmured, 'OK,' and tried hard not to notice that Terri was gaping at her like a startled fish.

Quickly, Mario rubbed the defibrillating paddles together with electrical conducting gel, shouted an urgent, 'Stand clear everyone,' then pressed the paddles hard on either side of Ewan Fraser's chest.

'Nothing,' Terri said, her eyes fixed on the monitor.

'Up the power,' he ordered, and Terri glanced across at Kate, who nodded her agreement, but it made no difference.

No matter how often Mario placed the paddles on Ewan Fraser's chest, the heart monitor remained resolutely flat, and after fifteen minutes Kate held up her hand.

'I'm calling it unless anybody has any other ideas?' she said, and both Terri and Mario shook their heads.

'Time of death, 15.45,' Terri murmured, then cleared her throat. 'His wife and son are outside in the family room, Kate.'

She wished they weren't, but breaking bad news to relatives was part of her job, and gently she touched Ewan Fraser's forehead with her fingers, murmured a farewell, then walked, stiff-backed, out of the cubicle.

'Do you always do that?' Marco asked curiously as he followed her. 'Say goodbye to a patient who's died?'

She coloured. 'I know it's stupid, but I always want them to know that I did my very best, that I didn't want to lose them, and I guess…I guess I also want to wish them godspeed. I know it makes no sense—'

'It makes perfect sense to me,' he interrupted, his voice husky, 'and I think it's nice.'

'In that case, do you want to hear something that really *is* stupid?' she said, fighting to keep her voice steady. 'I hate this moment—the moment before I go outside and break the bad news to the relatives. I always feel that if I stay in here—'

'His family will be able to hope for just a little bit longer,' he finished for her. 'Right now, they don't know that they're never going to hear his voice again, or see him smile, and you feel that if you stay in here they can keep on hoping—just for a little while longer—that everything will be all right whereas the minute you go out there you extinguish that hope and their lives are changed for ever.'

'How did you know that?' she said in surprise, and he smiled.

'Because I used to feel the same myself.'

'Did you?' she said, and when he nodded, her own lips curved into a lopsided smile. 'You're not as tough as you pretend, are you, Mario Volante?'

'Dammit, but I've been rumbled,' he replied in his usual, casual, jesting way, then quirked an eyebrow at her. 'You aren't, either, are you?'

'No. No, I'm not,' she murmured. 'I guess…I guess we're both frauds, deep down.'

He stretched out his hand and gently touched her cheek.

'At least you're a nice fraud, Kate. A kind fraud.'

And you don't know me at all, she thought, feeling her heart twist inside her as she gazed up at him. I'm not a nice person, not really. I get bad-tempered, and bitchy, and, when I do, I take it out on the people who love me, and then they walk away.

'What's wrong?' he asked, his eyes searching her face, and she shook her head.

'I just wish I was half as nice as you seem to think I am,' she replied, and his eyes gleamed.

'Of course you are. You're also crabby, and argumentative, and a downright pain in the butt at times, but then you wouldn't be Kate Elizabeth Kennedy if you weren't.'

She gazed at him uncertainly. 'Have you just paid me a compliment, or deeply insulted me?' she said and he grinned.

'Let me know when you've figured it out, and then I'll know when to duck.'

And she laughed properly this time but, as he strode across the treatment room in answer to one of the unit nurses' beckoning wave, her laughter slowly faded. What did he want from her? She was damned if she knew. She thought he liked her, and she knew she liked him, but all this teasing, all this trying to make her laugh… Was he just an incorrigible flirt who couldn't resist trying it on with any woman, or did it mean more?

Do you want it to mean more? her mind whispered, and she sighed.

Part of her said, yes, that it would be fun to go out with a man like Mario Volante, but the other part, the hurt part, the bewildered part that John had left behind when he'd walked away, warned that Mario could hurt her a lot more than her ex-husband ever had.

'I've cleared away all the equipment,' Terri declared as she joined her, 'and made Mr Fraser look as unmarked as I can.'

'Thanks, Terri.' Kate nodded, and stiffened her spine.

She couldn't put off breaking the bad news to Ewan Fraser's family any longer. It had to be done, she knew it had, just as she also had a niggling suspicion that this was going to turn out to be a spectacularly rotten day.

She was right. They had two MVAs in quick succession, and Terri collared her just before the end of her shift.

'OK, I want the truth about Mario Volante,' the sister declared, her bespectacled face determined, 'and I want it now.'

'I don't know what you mean,' Kate replied, all too aware that the wash of bright colour she could feel staining her cheeks was totally belying her words. 'He's an old friend from med school who's been nursing overseas—'

'Kate, if that guy is a nurse, I'm the Sugar Plum Fairy,' Terri interrupted. 'Who is he? *What* is he?'

Paul was watching them curiously from outside one of the cubicles, and Kate drew Terri further down the treatment room.

'OK, all right,' she began, wishing with all her heart that Mario hadn't been quite so insistent that nobody must know who he was. 'He's not an auxiliary nurse, he's a doctor.'

'Ah-*hah!*' Terri exclaimed, then her face creased in bewilderment. 'But if he's a doctor, what he's doing here as an auxiliary nurse?'

Good question.

'He hasn't practised as a doctor for eight years,' Kate replied. 'Because…um… There was an illness in his family, but now…now he wants to return to medicine, and Admin…' Oh, lord, but she hated lying to her friend, and she wasn't even making a very good job of it if Terri's raised eyebrows were anything to go by. 'Admin has agreed that he can work in A and E as an auxiliary nurse to see if…if that's really what he wants to do.'

It sounded lame. It sounded completely unbelievable, and Terri clearly thought so, too.

'But why is he pretending to be a *nurse?*' she demanded. 'Why can't he just tell everyone he used to be a doctor?'

Another good question.

'Because he…he's…' *Got a criminal record for GBH? Because he's an idiot who didn't realise that any experienced A and E sister would suss him out in a week?* 'Because—'

'Attempted suicide on the way in,' Colin interrupted. 'Seventeen-year-old female, ETA five minutes.'

Which was all she needed at the end of a long and weary shift, Kate thought as Terri raced away, but at least it had put an end to Terri's questions, though one glance at the sister's face had told her she was merely postponing the inevitable.

'Her mother found her fifteen minutes ago with an empty

paracetamol bottle and a half full bottle of vodka by her side,' the paramedic declared when Terri and Mario had carefully lifted the teenager onto the examination trolley.

'Did her mother say when she last spoke to her?' Kate asked.

'An hour ago—maybe a little longer.'

Which meant, with luck, the paracetamol should still be in the girl's stomach and they'd be able to pump it out using gastric lavage. It wasn't a pleasant procedure, but if the pills weren't extracted from the girl's stomach her liver would be irreparably damaged.

'Kate, look at this,' Terri muttered after they'd cut off the teenager's blouse and trousers.

The girl's arms and legs were covered with old scars and abrasions, and Kate groaned. Not only had the girl tried to commit suicide, she was also a self-cutter into the bargain.

'Why does anybody do that?' she said as Mario held the girl down while she inserted a large tube down her throat. 'I know people can become suicidal, but to physically cut yourself…'

'Some kids do it because they're being bullied at school, or because they're suffering physical and sexual abuse at home,' he replied. 'Others simply want to find out if anyone loves them, or to punish themselves for some perceived wrong-doing on their part.'

Kate shook her head. 'It's so sad—so very sad. At seventeen she should be going to parties, having fun, and to feel at that age your life is worth nothing…'

'A lot of people do,' Mario said, and something about his voice made her look up at him.

He was reliving some moment in his past. She didn't know how she knew that, but she did. There was raw pain in his face, the kind of pain she had never—thank God—experienced, but she couldn't say anything, not with Terri standing there.

'At least she's not a user,' she said tentatively instead. 'There are no track lines on her arms.'

'No,' he said tightly. 'Do you want sorbitol added to the charcoal?'

'IC will cut up rough if we use sorbitol,' Terri pointed out. 'You know how they prefer everything scrubbed and cleaned and sterile, and if we give this girl sorbitol she'll be anything but.'

'IC can whistle Dixie,' Kate declared firmly. 'Our job is to get as many of the pills out of her stomach as we can, so add the sorbitol.'

And they did, and the girl fought them all the way, so that by the time she had been transferred to IC not only was she covered in charcoal and sorbitol, Mario and Kate were, too.

'IC are definitely not going to be happy,' Mario observed as Kate threw her stained white coat into the laundry basket.

'IC are never happy with us,' Kate replied. 'As Terri said, they prefer everything clean and neat, and we…we…'

'We what?' he demanded as her voice trailed away into silence.

He'd peeled off his tunic top whilst she'd been talking and, oh, lord, but he had a beautiful chest. Broad, heavy muscled, and olive coloured with a slight sheen of sweat left from his attempts to keep the teenage girl from choking during the gastric lavage, it was the kind of chest that just cried out to be touched. The kind of chest that…

'Kate, we what?'

Quickly she tore her gaze away from his chest and stared fixedly at the laundry basket as though it was the most riveting thing in the world.

'W-we keep sending them all these messy, dirty, difficult patients,' she managed to say, and heard him exhale with exasperation.

'Dammit, it's their job—what they're paid for!' he exclaimed.

'I know, but…' She shot him a quick, uncertain glance only to immediately wish she hadn't.

He really did have a chest to die for. The sort of chest a girl could cling to. The sort of chest that was just asking to be caressed and kissed, and she wanted to be the one doing the caressing and kissing.

'Kate…?'

Damn, but he'd noticed her staring, and she waited for him to make some smart comment, but to her surprise he didn't. Instead he suddenly seemed to find the laundry basket just as interesting as she had done.

'You'll make sure the psychiatric staff talk to the girl once she's recovered?' he said, yanking a still-buttoned shirt quickly over his head. 'She'll probably need one-to-one monitoring for quite a while. And before you say it,' he added. 'I know that's an infringement of her personal liberty, but to hell with personal liberty if she does this again and kills herself.'

'I…um…I—I wasn't going to say it was an infringement,' she stammered. *Don't think about his chest, forget he has a chest, pull yourself together.* 'In cases like this, somebody's safety is more important than their civil liberties.'

'Yes.'

'Kids—young people,' she said tentatively. 'They really push your buttons, don't they?'

His face darkened. 'I don't like bad things happening to anybody.'

'No, but you especially don't like it when it happens to young people,' she pressed.

For a moment she thought he wasn't going to answer, then he nodded.

'Too many of them fall through the net, Kate!' he exclaimed. 'Too many of them die when if only somebody had listened to them, seen the warning signs, they might have pulled through.'

'Is that why you went into the drugs squad?' she asked. 'Did somebody you know fall through the net?'

'*Madre di Dio*, must you stick your damned nose into everything?'

His words had come out like a whiplash, and her mouth fell open with surprise.

'I wasn't sticking my nose in,' she protested. 'I was just concerned because that girl obviously upset you, and I thought—'

'I don't give a damn what you thought,' he flared. 'My private life is none of your business, so back off.'

'Back off?' she repeated. '*Back off?* So, what you're saying is that it's OK for you to know every small, personal detail about my private life, but not for me to know anything about yours, is that it?'

'I *have* to know about your private life,' he replied impatiently. 'You're a witness in a case I'm working on.'

'But I thought…' She cleared her throat. 'I thought we were friends, too.'

'Even if we were friends,' he exclaimed, 'that doesn't give you the right to poke and prod about in my private life!'

Even if they were friends?

'I wasn't poking and prodding!' she exclaimed. 'I just thought that as you're clearly upset, if you wanted to talk about it…I might be able to help.'

'I don't need any help,' he retorted.

'But it might help me to understand—'

'You don't need to understand anything about me.'

His face was cold, closed, and he couldn't have hurt her more if he'd actually slapped her.

'I see,' she said slowly, and she stared at him for a long moment, then nodded. 'Right. Fine.'

But it wasn't fine, she thought as she walked out of the treatment room, feeling both stupid and quite ridiculously close to tears at the same time. She was a fool, such a fool. Of course he was only here because he was working on a case, and she should have realised that all his flirting and teasing meant nothing. He probably flirted with every woman he met, and she'd been an idiot to think—hope?—that it might mean something, might lead somewhere.

OK, all right, she decided with a shuddering breath as she went into her office, made a quick phone call, then retrieved her handbag. She might be an idiot but that didn't mean she had to continue behaving like one. In future she'd ignore his teasing, and treat all his attempts to flirt with her with the contempt they so richly deserved. It was called survival.

'Mario's out front, waiting for you as usual,' Bill, the porter, called after her as she passed him, and she squared her shoulders.

Every night since Mario had started work at the General he had insisted on giving her a lift home at the end of her shift, and she'd given in because it was easier than arguing. Well, tonight was going to be different. Tonight he could go to hell, and with her head held high, she strode out of the hospital and straight past Mario's car without so much as giving it a second glance.

The result was predictable. She heard the sound of a car door slamming, followed by the thud of running feet, and the next minute Mario was standing in front of her, looking highly annoyed.

'Where the hell do you think you're going?' he demanded.

'Home,' she replied, trying to sidestep him without success.

'I always drive you home,' he declared, and she threw him a withering look.

'You have driven me home exactly five times,' she said. 'No way does that count as "always", and tonight I want to walk.'

'Then I'll walk with you.'

'I don't want you to walk with me!' she exclaimed, stepping to the left only to see him step to her left, to block her way.

'I don't care what you want,' he replied. 'You either get in the car and let me drive you home, or I'm walking with you.'

'And I don't care what *you* want,' she retorted, 'and if you don't get out of *my* way I am going to scream, "Rape," at the top of my lungs.'

'You wouldn't.'

'You think?' she said, meeting him glare for glare, and he was the one who looked away first.

'Kate, listen, I—' He raked his fingers through his black hair, and to her amazement he actually looked uncomfortable. 'What I said earlier—about you sticking your nose in—I shouldn't have said it.'

'Fine,' she said, 'and now will you please get out of my way?'

'*Madre di Dio*, Kate, I'm trying to hold out an olive branch here—to apologise,' he protested. 'Won't you at least meet me halfway, let me drive you home, or at least walk with you?'

She didn't want him to do either. If he drove her home she'd have to endure fifteen minutes of his company, and if he walked with her it would take at least forty-five minutes, but the night staff were beginning to arrive and the longer she stood there arguing with him, the more attention she would draw to herself.

'OK, you can drive me home,' she said, 'but don't think that means I'm going to talk to you, because I'm not.'

'Agreed,' he said. 'You can sit in silence and I'll drive and feel like the low life scum I undoubtedly am.'

Her lips twitched and ruthlessly she subdued them. No way was she going to forgive him. He had snubbed her—dammit, he'd told her they weren't even friends—so no way was she going to forgive him, but, as he drove her through the city streets, she very quickly discovered that sitting in complete silence was a lot harder than it had sounded.

'Do you mind if we have some music?' she said.

'Not at all,' he said, his voice every bit as formal as hers.

Was he laughing at her? If he was laughing at her she'd make him sorry, but his face was perfectly bland, and, quickly, she punched the buttons on his car radio to discover there was nothing but football, football, and more football on all the channels. OK, so it was Saturday night, but why was there never any music on the radio when a girl needed music?

'I have a CD player,' he observed, clearly reading her mind.

And it had a CD in it, she noticed, so she hit the play button with relief only to sit, horror-stricken, as the sound of Johnny Cash's deep and gravelly voice rang out.

For a long moment she said nothing, then cleared her throat.

'You like Johnny Cash,' she said awkwardly, and he nodded.

'Yup, I do.'

'Then why didn't you say so when those line dancers were in earlier in the week?' she demanded, and he glanced across at her.

'Well, you seemed to be on such a roll with your diatribe against country and western music that it seemed a pity to interrupt you.'

'I'm sorry,' she said, her voice small.

'Sorry because you now feel highly embarrassed, or sorry because you made such a gross generalisation?'

'It must be nice to be always in the right,' she said tightly, and he shot her another glance.

'And that is not an answer.'

'OK, I'm embarrassed!' she exclaimed. 'And OK, I made a bit of a generalisation.'

'A bit?'

'All right—a lot,' she said through her teeth. 'Satisfied now?'

Dammit, but he'd wrong-footed her again, she thought, seeing the all too familiar quirk at his lips. *She* was the aggrieved party here, the one who had been well and truly snubbed for suggesting they might be friends, and now she felt in the wrong. How the hell was she supposed to have guessed he might be a country and western fan? It would never have occurred to her in a million years.

Which is why I really *must* start distancing myself from him, she told herself as she gazed stonily out of the car window. I know nothing about him, and now I've discovered he likes country and western music. OK, so it's hardly a major thing on the Richter scale of likes and dislikes, but at least John and I shared the same taste in music.

Much good it did you, her mind pointed out, considering he left you.

OK, all right, she argued back, but at least John *wanted* to get involved with me. Mario doesn't. I'm just a case to him—he said so—and even if he was interested if I couldn't make a go of it with a man who wanted nothing more from me, than myself and a family, what hope would I have of succeeding with a man who is as driven and argumentative as I am?

'Kate, I truly am sorry for what I said.'

There was deep regret in Mario's voice and she turned slowly to face him but he wasn't looking at her. He was looking at the road ahead, and a muscle was clenched tight at the side of his cheek.

'We *are* friends,' he continued, 'and I shouldn't have accused you of being nosy. You were just trying to help.'

'Are you going to tell me why you reacted as you did?' she said. 'Explain why you got so angry?'

The muscle in his cheek tightened even more.

'Not today. I will tell you one day, but not today.'

It was another olive branch—sort of—and she could take it, or she could tell him what she knew she ought. That him telling her 'one day' wasn't good enough and that she wanted him to get the hell out of her life and leave her alone.

But she didn't say that.

'OK,' she heard herself say, and knew she was weak and feeble, but, as his eyes met hers, and his lips curved into a warm smile, she also knew—dispiritingly—that she didn't care.

'I'll walk you to your door,' he said when he drew his car to a halt outside her home.

'There's no need,' she replied, but he was already heading towards the passenger door and she sighed.

Maybe one day he might actually do as she asked.

Maybe.

'I telephoned IC before I left the hospital to ask about the teenager who overdosed,' she said when he took her arm and began steering her up her garden path.

'How's she doing?'

'Not out of the woods by a long way, but the signs are looking good. IC said…'

She never did get to finish what she'd been about to say. Dimly, she heard the sound of a car backfiring, and the next moment she was flat on her back on the scrubby grass in front of her home, and Mario was lying on top of her.

'What the hell do you think you're doing?' she exclaimed, and when he didn't answer she pushed as hard as she could against his chest but she might as well have been trying to move a boulder. 'Get off me!'

'Shut up.'

'*What?*' she exclaimed, incensed. 'Look, just because I said we were friends doesn't mean you can start behaving like some sort of…of Neanderthal pervert.'

'Somebody just took a shot at you.'

She rolled her eyes heavenwards, and counted to ten, but it didn't help.

'Mario, it was a car backfiring.'

'Somebody just took a shot at you,' he repeated. 'Quite close—maybe a hundred yards away.'

'Who in the world would want to shoot me?' she protested, wriggling to try to get out from under him then stopping quickly because it felt way too good. 'I'm a doctor, for God's sake.'

'They didn't intend to kill you,' he murmured. 'If they'd wanted you dead you'd have a bullet hole in your back right now. This was a warning. My guess is it was probably a .308 semi-automatic. Maybe a Bullmaster or a Panther.'

'And I expect the gun was also blue, with a pink handle, and played "Yankee Doodle Dandy",' she said, unable to hide her sarcasm. 'Mario, get a grip. This is Aberdeen, not New York.'

He wasn't even listening to her. He was searching the grass beside them with his eyes, then he stretched over, and picked something up. 'I'm not an expert—'

'Oh, wow, but we've found something you're *not* an expert on?'

'—but I think this is a 168-grain Ballistic Silvertip.'

She didn't know what make it was but even she knew that the object he was holding was a bullet and her stomach clenched tight for a second then sanity reasserted itself.

'OK, so somebody took a shot at us, but surely it's more likely they were shooting at you?' she declared.

'Kate—'

'You're in the drugs squad,' she continued, talking over him. 'You go after the bad guys, and if I were a bad guy the person I'd want to…to take out would be you.'

'Take out?' he repeated, a glimmer of laughter lighting up his eyes. 'You've been watching too many TV shows.'

'Laugh as much as you want,' she retorted, 'but it makes sense.'

He shook his head. 'Kate, maybe I should have told you this before, but the names Hamilton gave you—you could send down three of the biggest drug dealers in the business.'

He wasn't lying. She could see in his eyes that he was telling her the truth, but, even as a wave of icy fear began to twist its way around her heart, her mind went into denial. She was ordinary Kate Kennedy. A consultant at the General in Aberdeen and things like this didn't happen to her. They happened to other people. Important people who lived in New York or Chicago, not to somebody who lived in a faded, rundown back-street of Aberdeen.

'You're wrong,' she said, shaking her head as though by so doing she could make it true. 'OK, so I know all those names, but nobody else but you knows that I know them so nobody can be after me, they simply can't.'

'And yet they are,' he said simply, and try as she might she couldn't stop the wave of fear returning.

Desperately, she strained her ears to see if she could hear anybody moving nearby, but all she could hear was the distant rumble of traffic and the sound of somebody's radio from a house across the street.

'Where…?' She swallowed convulsively. 'Where do you think he is?'

'Who?'

'The tooth fairy,' she hissed in exasperation. 'The gunman, of course.'

'Oh, he'll be long gone by now,' Mario replied. 'As I said, I don't think he was trying to kill you, just to scare you.'

'Then why are we still lying on the ground?' she asked, and he grinned.

'Because, like you said, I'm a Neanderthal pervert.'

Not a pervert, she thought, as she gazed up at him open mouthed for a second, then started to laugh, but a very sexy man. An exceptionally sexy man but, as he continued to gaze down at her, her laughter gradually died as his smile slowly faded. He was all wrong for her—common sense told her he was—but common sense didn't prevent her heart from picking up speed when he gently brushed her hair back from her face with his fingers. Neither did it stop her body from responding when he shifted his weight slightly, and she felt the whole length of his hard muscular body against hers.

Did he feel it, too, she wondered, this intense physical awareness? She knew his breath had quickened. She knew his heart rate had increased, just as hers had done, because she could feel it through her blouse, and when he lowered his head her breath jammed in her throat. Was he going to kiss her? She very much hoped that he was going to kiss her, but, to her dismay, he suddenly stood up, leaving her feeling cold and bereft.

'Kate, I want you to do something for me,' he said, holding out his hand to help her up.

'What?' she said, ignoring his outstretched hand and scrambling to her feet herself, cursing herself for the overwhelming wave of disappointment she could feel.

'I want you to stay off work,' he replied. 'You can catch up on your reading, use the time to redecorate, surf eBay for bargains, do whatever you want, but I want you to stay home.'

'Mario, we've been through this before, and you know I can't,' she exclaimed in exasperation. 'I'm the consultant, I'm needed.'

'Nobody is indispensable.'

'Well, I am,' she retorted.

'Kate—'

'If you're right, and somebody really *is* trying to kill me,' she interrupted, hearing the slight wobble in her voice and despising herself for it, 'then they're going to get me no matter where I am.'

'Not if you stay in your flat, and don't open the door,' he declared, irritation plain in his voice, and she shook her head.

'I am not staying home, and that's final.'

'OK, I've tried asking you nicely,' he declared, clearly at the end of his patience, 'and now I'm ordering you to stay home.'

She gazed at him, outraged. 'You can't order me to do anything.'

'You think?' he said, his face suddenly furious. 'If you won't stay off work, and stay home, I'll book you.'

'What for?' she protested. 'I haven't done anything.'

'How about obstructing the police, putting yourself in danger, getting right up my nose?'

'That's blackmail,' she declared. 'What you're doing is blackmail, and I won't stand for it. I won't let—'

'*Dio! Dammi forza!*' he thundered, and her eyes narrowed.

'Are you swearing at me? If you're swearing at me...'

'No, I'm not swearing at you, though heaven knows you deserve it!' he exclaimed. 'Kate, you can argue until you're blue in the face, but it's not going to make any difference. You stay home. You don't open the door to anybody, you don't go near any windows, and you don't go to work. End of discussion.'

'But, if I never go out, how am I supposed to manage for food?' she demanded, clutching at straws. 'Or hadn't you thought of that?'

'Give me a list of the groceries you'll need, and I'll pick them up for you,' he replied. 'Or, if you'd prefer it I can ask one of our female officers to do it for you. I expect you'll have personal shopping—things you'd probably rather I didn't buy—'

'Oh, for crying out loud,' she interrupted. 'I don't care what you buy me, I just don't want to stay home.'

'But you will,' he replied, in a voice that told her there was no point in arguing, but she still intended to.

'This is payback time, isn't it?' she said. 'Payback because you think I'm a nosy snoop.'

'*Madre di Dio!*'

'Will you stop shouting at me in Italian?' she declared as he dragged his fingers through his hair in exasperation. 'If you're going to shout at me, then at least shout at me in a language I can understand.'

'This is *not* payback for this afternoon,' he said, clearly controlling his temper with difficulty. 'Look, I know you're mad as hell with me,' he continued as she tried to interrupt, 'but this is for your own safety. I don't want to have to identify you on a morgue slab.'

'You're overreacting—'

'But you will stay home.'

His blue eyes were as cold and as implacable as ice and she glared at him for a second, then turned on her heel and strode up her drive, but when she reached her front door she whirled round to face him.

'My life was simple—peaceful—until you came into it,' she yelled. 'And as far as I'm concerned, the sooner you're out of it, the better.'

Her life had been simple, he thought, as she slammed the door in his face. What about *his* life?

All he'd had to worry about before he'd met her had been his job, and making the monthly repayments on his flat, and now he was stuck with the witness from hell. A stroppy, opinionated, irritating woman, who wouldn't do as she was told even if her actual life depended on it. Dammit, didn't she realise that his whole case hinged on her being able to testify?

And is that the only reason you're insisting she stays home? his mind whispered, and he swore, long, and low, and fluently.

OK, so he couldn't deny he found her attractive when she wasn't yelling at him, but he couldn't get involved with her, simply couldn't. It wasn't just that his track record with women was lousy. He was too busy, had too much on his plate, and they were too different. *Dio mio!* She didn't even like Johnny Cash, and that should have told him something. Except…

'*Basta!*' he muttered as he strode towards his car, kicking at a stone that was stupid enough to get in his way.

Kate was right. The sooner he was out of her life, the better.

CHAPTER FIVE

IT WAS amazing the amount of work you could get through in a week if you had no interruptions, harassment, or phone calls, Mario thought, as he hit the save button on his computer then stretched his arms out in front of him to ease the knot he could feel between his shoulder blades. OK, so he still had rather a large backlog of paperwork to complete but, in general, everything was going well.

Really well, he decided, as he reached for his cup of coffee and his glance fell on the phone. He'd put Jason and Richard on a round-the-clock rotation watch of Kate's flat and they'd confirmed she was staying home as he'd ordered, so there was no need for him to speak to her. No need at all, especially when the one time he *had* phoned her she'd subjected him to an earful then put the phone down on him.

Yup, everything was just great. Kate might be furious, but at least she was safe, and as for him not seeing her or talking to her... It meant he could get on with his work, get his own life back together again, instead of wasting time babysitting a cranky consultant.

Except...

Dio, but he missed her. Missed her ready laugh and her flashing grey eyes, but he had to stop missing her. Relationships didn't work, not for him. Even on his wedding day he'd known he was making a mistake. Known he should have stopped it, but he'd gone ahead, and been forced to watch the love in Sue's eyes gradually being replaced by hurt and bitterness during their short marriage, and Kate deserved better than that. She deserved a man who could commit, a man who would be there for her, not a man who hadn't been whole for a very long time.

'Is that last night's dinner, or today's lunch?' Ralph Evanton asked, as he came into the office carrying a sheaf of folders and caught sight of the remains of some chicken madras congealing in a styrofoam container on the edge of Mario's desk.

'Can't remember,' Mario replied. 'And if you've come in here simply to bitch at me,' he continued as his detective sergeant shook his head at him, 'you can turn right around and walk out again.'

'Proper little ray of sunshine these days, aren't you?'

'Ralph...'

'OK—OK.' His detective sergeant grinned. 'Di Angelis, Faranelli and Mackay are still going about their daily lives as though they haven't got a care in the world.'

'And Hamilton's cutter?' Mario said, staring unseeing at his computer screen. 'Has he talked yet?'

'Not a squeak. My guess is he's more frightened of the big boys than he is of us sending him down for a long stretch.'

'Which means Kate is still our only witness.' Mario sighed. 'And if this ever gets to court—which I have to say I'm seriously beginning to doubt—the defence will make mincemeat of her evidence. They'll say she can't possibly remember names given to her while she was trying to save a dying man's life, and that will be that. Case dismissed.'

'But somebody took a shot at her,' Ralph declared. 'Surely that must count for something?'

'Not when the bullet could have been fired by anyone,' Mario replied. 'It's not looking good, Ralph, not good at all. In fact, the only thing I'm happy about is knowing Kate is safe at home.'

'Um… You might want to rethink that one,' Ralph observed uncomfortably, and Mario swung round fast in his seat.

'*Dio mio*, if she's gone back to work against my express orders—'

'She hasn't gone back to work,' Ralph interrupted, 'but Jason and Richard… They've both requested transfers. Actually what they said was you can assign them to the schools' drug programme for the duration for all they care, but they just can't watch over her any more. If she's not attempting to sneak past them, she's chewing their ears off for keeping her under surveillance.'

'I see.'

'Look, Jason and Richard have done their best,' Ralph exclaimed as he watched his boss unhook his leather jacket from the back of his chair. 'It isn't their fault.'

'I know it isn't,' Mario replied grimly. 'It's Kate. The only language that blasted woman understands is if you give it to her with both barrels.'

'OK, I'll go round to her place, have a word with her,' Ralph said, and Mario shook his head.

'*I'll* go. She'll just run rings round you.' He yanked opened the office door only to suddenly realise his detective sergeant was staring at him with a particularly annoying expression on his face. 'What?' he demanded. '*What?*'

'Nothing,' Ralph replied. 'Nothing at all.'

Mario stood in the centre of Kate's living room, his face livid with anger.

'Do you have *any* idea how much trouble you are causing by your refusal to obey one single, simple order?' he demanded, and Kate gazed back at him, as bright and shining as the mid-August sunshine and completely unrepentant.

'Mario, I'm going nuts cooped up in here.'

'Would anybody notice?' he exclaimed.

'Oh, *very* clever,' she said. 'If I watch any more daytime soaps I'll be certified as brain dead.'

'Better certified as brain dead than *actually* dead,' he threw back at her, trying hard not to notice that she looked just as gorgeous as he'd imagined she would with her hair lying loose on her shoulders. 'Kate, you are in danger. D-A-N-G-E-R.'

'You don't know that for sure,' she protested. 'In fact, the more I've thought about it, the more rational it seems to me that *you* were the target.'

'Kate—'

'Think about it, Mario. You're a drugs squad cop, I'm a doctor. I might irritate some people—'

'Put me at the top of that list.'

'But how realistic is it that somebody would want to kill me?'

'Continue to badger my men the way you've been doing, and *I'll* kill you!' he exclaimed. 'Kate, I had to take Jason and Richard off other important cases to protect you, and how have you repaid them? By constantly trying to sneak past them to get back to the unit and when they try to stop you, you chew them out in the street—using language, I might add, that would make a docker blush—and all because you're a little bored.'

'I'm not *a little* bored, Mario,' she said. 'I'm wall-climbing, head-banging bored. Nothing has happened to me—'

'Only because you've stayed indoors.' His forehead pleated as he caught sight of a pile of oddly shaped parcels heaped at the side of her sofa. 'What's all this?'

'You told me to surf eBay, so I did. I've bought three lamps, four pairs of shoes, two sweaters and a coat. If I stay home much longer I'll be bankrupt.'

And he was going to have some very severe words with Jason and Richard, Mario decided grimly, as he stared down at the packages. Any one of those parcels could contain explosives, and yet neither Jason nor Richard had examined them before allowing them to be delivered.

'Kate, listen to me. I…'

He stopped abruptly. She'd uncurled herself from the sofa and stood up and, *Dio*, but the jeans she was wearing were hip-hugging. Extremely hip-hugging, and the way her blue sweater was clinging to her breasts…

'…if it was you?' she said, and he shook his head to clear it.

'If it was me what?' he asked.

'I *said*, would you stay home, if it was you?' she demanded, and he gritted his teeth impatiently.

'Being threatened by these sorts of low life scum is an occupational hazard for me,' he replied. 'It's part of my job, but you're a woman. You're…'

He came to a halt as a martial glint appeared in her eyes. It had been the wrong thing to say, and he'd known it the minute the words were out of his mouth.

'Kate—'

'So li'l ol' me can't cope, is that what you're saying?' she said dangerously. 'Li'l ol' me has to be shut away in solitary confinement because I can't hack it. Well, let me tell you this, mister, I'm going back to work this afternoon, and you'll have to clap me in irons to stop me.'

'And you think that can't be arranged?' he declared, every bit as angry now as she was, and for a moment he thought she was going to argue with him, then her lips twisted slightly.

'Mario, I know you think I'm stupid. I know you're just trying to protect me, but I *have* to go back to work. You've been a doctor. You know what it's like. There's never enough staff, never enough pairs of hands, and you've seen how grossly understaffed my department is. People *need* me, and I can't let them down, I simply can't.'

'I appreciate that, Kate, I do, but don't you understand that this isn't a game?' he protested. 'This isn't a film where people pretend to get shot then get up and go home at the end of the filming. You could *die*.'

'I know.' She nodded. 'But the thing is, it really wouldn't matter if I did, would it?'

'*In nome di Dio*, Kate—'

'I'm not angling for sympathy here,' she said quickly, as he gazed at her, appalled, 'but let's look at the facts. I'm not married, I don't have any children, or brothers and sisters, my parents are both dead, so it's not as though…' She smiled a little crookedly. 'It's not as though I'd be leaving anyone bereft if anything happened to me. The only person I have to worry about is myself and, for me, the risk is worth taking.'

But it's not worth taking for me, he thought, as his eyes met hers. If anything should happen to her… If he never saw her laugh again, or smelt her perfume, or saw her chew her lip when she was thinking… But he couldn't tell her that, hated admitting it even to himself.

'OK,' he said slowly, 'if you must go back to work, then I'll let you. But,' he continued as her large grey eyes lit up with clear delight, 'there are conditions. You have to let me come back and work in your department—'

'Not a problem.'

'—and you have to let me move in with you.'

'I have to *what?*' she exclaimed.

'You heard me. Kate, you have as much sense when it comes to your own safety as a toddler wielding a blowtorch, so I want to be there when you're at work, and here when you get home so you don't open the door and invite every conman and low life villain there is into your house.'

Not to mention a whole load of parcels that could contain anything, he thought, his eyes sliding to the stack in the corner.

'But you can't move in—there's no room,' she declared. 'This is a one-bedroomed flat.'

'You have a couch.'

She did, but Kate wasn't at all sure that she wanted him sleeping on it. Dammit, she was all too aware of how attracted to him she was, and to have him living with her... What if she did something stupid? What if she threw herself at him, and he knocked her back? What if she threw herself at him, and he *didn't* knock her back, and she lived to regret it for the rest of her life?

'That's the deal, Kate,' Mario continued, watching her. 'Take it, or leave it because it's non-negotiable.'

Oh, hell. She had to go back to work—simply had to—but...

She took a deep breath. OK, all right. She could do this. She was thirty-four years old—thirty-five in a fortnight—she could manage it. She'd be at work all day, and when she came home she could bring paperwork with her, immerse herself in that, have lots of baths, very early nights...

'OK, it's a deal,' she said in a rush. 'Give me fifteen minutes to get changed, and then I'll be ready.'

'For what?' he said, puzzled, as she made for the sitting room door.

'Going back to work, of course,' she replied.

'*Now?*' he exclaimed. 'Kate, it's six o'clock—'

'Which means I've only missed two hours of the evening shift,' she said, and as she disappeared into her bedroom, she didn't see him raise his eyes heavenwards and mutter something unprintable under his breath.

'So, how are you feeling?' Terri asked, her eyes fixed on Kate sympathetically. 'I mean, *really* feeling?'

'Fine, thank you,' Kate replied, wondering what on earth Mario had told everyone as she slipped on her white coat.

'That flu bug is really debilitating, isn't it?' Terri declared, un-
wittingly coming to her rescue. 'And I have to say I think you
still look a bit peaky.'

Probably because I haven't seen daylight for a week, Kate
thought, wondering what else Mario might have told the staff in
A and E and wishing he'd remembered to fill her in.

Not that she'd actually given him any time to fill her in, she
thought with a wry inward chuckle, as she saw him deep in conversation with Colin. She'd virtually pushed him out of her flat,
and he'd grumbled all the way here.

'How have things been in the unit this past week?' she asked,
deliberately changing the subject. 'Did Paul hold the fort OK?'

'Hold the fort?' Terri echoed. 'Kate, he's being running the
place like a boot camp. Do this, do that. Poor Colin was telling
me only last night that he was thinking of throwing in the towel.'

'That bad?' Kate observed, and Terri made an expressive
slicing motion across her own throat.

'And then some. Of course, it didn't help that we were so
terribly short-staffed—no criticism of you meant,' the sister added,
'but what with Mario going down with the same bug as you—'

'He did?'

'A really bad dose, apparently.' Terri nodded. 'Which reminds
me,' she continued, leaning forward, her eyes gleaming, 'we
never did finish our conversation about him.'

And I really don't want to finish it now, Kate thought, wondering if she could possibly fake a suddenly remembered, urgent
meeting, but she didn't have to.

'Excuse me, ladies,' a deep male voice interrupted, and Kate
turned to see an absolutely enormous strange man pushing an
empty wheelchair down the treatment room.

'Who's that?' she asked when the man had passed, and Terri
rolled her eyes.

'Our new porter.'

'Our new… What happened to Bill?' Kate protested. 'If Men's Surgical have poached him from us—'

'No, they haven't poached him. Bill phoned in the day after you went off sick to say he'd got an unexpected windfall so he was off to New Zealand to see his granddaughter.'

'Oh. Right. Terrific. For him I mean,' Kate murmured. Damnation, she'd only been gone a week and suddenly the unit didn't feel like it was hers any more. 'So, what's he called—this new porter?'

'The incredible hulk.'

Kate let out a spurt of laughter. 'No, seriously, what's his name?'

'George Luciano.'

The incredible hulk suited him better, Kate decided, but never would she have said so.

'One thing's for sure,' she said instead as she watched George manoeuvre his wheelchair between the cubicles as though it weighed no more than a feather. 'He's certainly going to put the fear of God into our Saturday night drunks.'

'I don't know about the drunks, but he definitely gives me the creeps,' Terri declared.

Me, too, Kate thought, feeling a prickle of unease when the new porter stopped at the bottom of the treatment room and turned to stare back at her. Not staring in a 'Wow, but that woman's gorgeous' sort of a way, or a 'Yikes, but that woman really should lose some weight' kind of way, but simply staring.

Hadn't there been a man called 'Lucky' Luciano who had been one of the most notorious of the old time Mafia bosses in America in the early years of the twentieth century? Maybe George was a descendant. Maybe he was a hit man sent by the Mafia to get her.

And maybe she should just pull herself together, she told herself irritably. George Luciano was probably nothing more than a very large man who was interested in everything that happened in an A and E unit. A lot of new porters were, and she probably wouldn't even have noticed him—well, not much at any rate—if Mario hadn't encouraged her to see danger lurking at every corner.

'Ah, Kate, good to see you back again,' Paul Simpson declared, striding towards her with an expression that suggested he felt it was anything but. 'I've been keeping everything ticking over for you, keeping detailed spreadsheets of every patient we've seen, so if you would care to check them…?'

He had to be kidding. If he thought she wanted to spend her first evening back in the unit gazing at spreadsheets then he don't know her. Which he didn't.

'I'm afraid that much as I'd like to go through the spreadsheets with you, Paul,' she said sweetly, 'duty calls.'

'Duty?' he repeated, clearly puzzled, and she gestured towards Mario who was coming towards them accompanied by a young woman carrying a toddler.

'Patients, Paul,' she declared. 'Remember them?'

And before Paul could mention the zillion memos he'd had to deal with from Admin, or the problems he'd had with the laundry inventory, she strode quickly towards the young mother with a smile.

'Mrs Judy Lowell,' Mario explained. 'Her hand slipped when she was cutting some bread, and she's sustained rather a nasty cut to her thumb.'

'I feel so *stupid!* 'Mrs Lowell exclaimed as Kate ushered her into cubicle 4. 'Jack was getting into everything as usual, and I was watching him because he *will* put things in his mouth, and the next thing I knew the knife hit my hand, and there was blood everywhere, and Jack was screaming, so I thought I'd better come down here right away.'

'Very wise,' Kate observed, as she gently unwrapped the bloodstained tea towel that the young mother had wrapped round her hand. 'Oh, ouch, but that *is* a nasty one,' she added as she reached for the antiseptic cleaner. 'So, Jack's rather lively, is he?'

'You can say that again,' Judy Lowell replied ruefully. 'He's only three, but ever since he started to walk I've needed eyes at the back of my head.'

Kate laughed as she looked down at the little boy who gazed back at her with huge, angelic brown eyes.

'And there was me thinking he looked as though butter wouldn't melt in his mouth.'

'Don't you believe it, Doctor!' Judy Lowell exclaimed. 'I swear I've aged twenty years since I had him. Have you kids yourself?' she added, glancing from Kate to Mario. 'Either of you?'

'No, we don't,' Kate said quickly, remembering what had happened the last time anyone—OK, so it was her—had asked Mario whether he had children. 'I'm afraid this is definitely going to need stitches,' she continued. 'Four—maybe even five. Nurse Volante…'

Mario was already holding out a syringe to her, and she smiled. It was *so* good to be back. She hadn't been exaggerating when she'd said she'd been mind-numbingly bored at home. No matter what she'd done—whether it had been watching TV, reading or surfing the net—she'd found herself constantly thinking about the unit, wondering what was happening, what she was missing, and to be back was heaven, pure heaven.

'If you could put your son down on the floor for me for a few minutes, Mrs Lowell,' she said, 'I promise all you'll feel is a tiny pinprick in your hand and then, once the anaesthetic has taken effect, I'll be able to stitch your thumb and you'll be on your way.'

'If you say so, Doctor,' the young mother muttered, gazing apprehensively at the syringe, and Mario smiled encouragingly at her.

'Hey, relax. We haven't lost a patient yet.'

'Maybe not, but there's always a first time,' Judy Lowell

observed. She put her son down and fixed him with a stern gaze. 'Be a good boy for Mummy, Jack, and *don't* touch anything.'

'He'll be fine,' Kate said reassuringly, as she inserted the anaesthetic into the young woman's hand. 'There's not a lot in here he can find interesting.'

'That's what I thought when I took him to Inverness on the train last week,' Judy Lowell replied, 'and he still managed to lock himself in the train toilet. They had to take the door off to get him out.'

Kate laughed. 'He sounds like a real livewire.' She prodded gently at Mrs Lowell's hand, and nodded. 'That looks nicely numb to me. Nurse Volante…?'

She hadn't needed to ask. Mario was already holding out the needle and suturing thread to her, and with a smile of thanks she took them from him.

'You don't have an Aberdonian accent, Mrs Lowell,' she declared, deliberately making conversation to help put the young mother at her ease while she sutured her thumb. 'Where are you from?'

'Yorkshire, originally,' Judy Lowell replied, 'but my husband works in the oil industry so we had to relocate here.'

'Does he work offshore?' Kate asked, and Mrs Lowell nodded.

'Quite what he's going to say about my hand… Jack, put that bottle cap down. Jack, no—*not in your mouth.*'

Kate whirled round quickly, but she was too late. The bottle cap had disappeared and Jack was smiling up at them, completely unconcerned.

'Spit it out, Jack,' Mario declared, his voice deliberately casual, his hand outstretched, but Jack didn't.

In fact, Jack was beginning to gulp, and choke, quite alarmingly.

'Oh, my God,' Mrs Lowell shrieked, sending the tray of instruments which Mario had left beside her flying. *'Do something!'*

Mario did. Quickly, he put his finger inside the child's mouth.

'Can't feel it,' he muttered, then knelt down, put the little boy across his thighs, and administered five firm blows to the middle of the toddler's back.

Nothing happened. The bottle top was clearly wedged tight in Jack's windpipe and his breath was coming in increasingly wheezy gasps.

'*Oh, my God*,' Mrs Lowell cried. 'He's choking—*he's choking!*'

Again, Mario hit the toddler squarely in the centre of his back and, to Kate's relief, with a cough, and a splutter, the bottle cap suddenly shot out of Jack's mouth and landed on the floor.

'We have a result,' Mario declared, smiling up at Mrs Lowell, and she promptly burst into tears.

'I don't know what to say,' she sobbed. 'How to thank you, Doctor—'

'Nurse, actually.'

'You were wonderful—just wonderful,' Mrs Lowell continued. 'If I weren't a married woman, I'd kiss you.'

'Well, I won't tell, if you don't,' Mario said, his eyes gleaming, and Kate laughed, and Mrs Lowell laughed, and Jack looked thoroughly confused.

'Well done on the quick reflexes,' Kate said once she'd finished stitching Mrs Lowell's hand and the young mother and her son had gone safely on their way.

'All in a day's work,' he replied airily. 'Mario Volante, leaper of tall buildings in a single bound, rescuer of cats stuck up trees, saviour of small children in distress.'

'And cleaner up of cubicle 4 which now looks as though a bomb has hit it,' Kate replied, her lips twitching, and he looked outraged.

'Superman never got this,' he protested, and she laughed and shook her head and shooed him, still grumbling, back into cubicle 4.

What was it about him that she liked so much? she wondered as she erased Judy Lowell's name from the whiteboard. OK, so he was good-looking, and he made her laugh, but she'd met other men who had been able to do the same and none of them had ever been able to reach her in quite the way Mario had. What was it that was so different about him? She was damned if she knew, and, with a sigh, she turned to see who was next on the list only to frown slightly as she watched a middle-aged man walk slowly towards the treatment room door, then turn to stare back at her, looking distinctly disgruntled.

'Terri,' she said slowly as the sister passed her. 'That man who's just leaving—hasn't he been in before?'

'You examined him about ten days ago. His name's Stewart Bolton, and he came in with food poisoning on the same day as all those other people with food poisoning. Paul reckons he's a bounce-back.'

Maybe he was, Kate thought, as she watched the man leave, but bounce-backs didn't usually come in complaining of food poisoning. They presented with much vaguer, woollier symptoms that could have fitted any amount of conditions.

'Did he come in with the same symptoms?' she asked. 'Sickness, vomiting, diarrhoea?'

'Yup, but now he's added dizzy spells, and feeling "just plain odd" to his list. He also seemed less than pleased to have Paul examining him.'

Kate's frown deepened. That was unusual, too. Bounce-backs were normally delighted to see as many different doctors as possible because then there was less likelihood of them being told there was nothing wrong with them, but this man hadn't been happy.

'If he presents again, I want to see him,' she said. 'He probably *is* just a bounce-back, but I'd like to take another look at him just to make sure.'

'Not a problem,' Terri declared, then leant forward, her eyes sparkling. 'Now, you were going to finish what you were telling me about Mario.'

Was she? Kate couldn't remember promising she would, but she couldn't see any way out of it. Terri wouldn't give her a minute's peace until she told her the truth, and while Mario had forbidden her to tell anybody anything she was certain—OK, make that ninety-nine per cent certain—that he hadn't meant to include one of her oldest and closest friends.

'OK, I'll tell you the truth,' Kate declared, glancing over her shoulder to make sure no one was listening. 'But you mustn't tell anybody what I'm going to tell you because it's very hush-hush, and you most definitely mustn't tell Mario that you know.'

'OK—OK,' Terri said impatiently. 'Now, give.'

'Mario… He used to be a doctor,' Kate said, 'but now he's a policeman. An inspector to be exact, in the drugs squad. He's working undercover on a case here, but I can't tell you any more than that.'

'Oh, *wow*,' Terry breathed, her eyes round. 'Frank is never going to believe this. When I tell him—'

'Terri, you can't tell your husband—you can't tell *anybody*,' Kate interrupted quickly. 'As I said it's top secret.'

'Well, he can't be investigating somebody in our department,' Terri murmured as though Kate hadn't spoken, 'because I check the drug cupboard every day, and nothing's ever been missing.'

'Terri—'

'It's Duncan Hamilton, isn't it?' Terri said with sudden triumph. 'Mario's here because of that body-packer, isn't he?'

'You didn't hear that from me,' Kate declared, beginning to panic. 'I never said—'

'Oh, Kate, this is *so* exciting.'

You don't know the half of it, Kate thought grimly.

She fervently wished she didn't either as the evening wore on and every time she looked up it was to find either Terri staring at her, clearly still agog with what she'd revealed, Paul looking as though somebody had just stolen his favourite toy, or their new porter's eyes boring into her. In fact, the only person who didn't seem to feel the need to stare at her was Mario, and she wasn't altogether sure whether that was a good thing or not.

'Tired?' Mario asked when their shift was eventually over and Kate wearily went into her office to retrieve her handbag.

'A bit,' she admitted.

'Just as well we're going home, then, isn't it?' he said, and she smiled back only for her smile to slide slowly sideways as the implication of his words sank in.

He meant home, as in her home. Home as in the two of them sharing her tiny one-bedroomed flat for goodness knew how long. OK, so she'd agreed to it this afternoon, but she hadn't really thought it through. Not properly.

'Won't you need to go back to your place first to collect some of your belongings?' she said hopefully, and he shook his head.

'I phoned Ralph when I got into the hospital this afternoon, and he nipped round to my flat, packed a bag for me, and brought it round to Reception about an hour ago.'

Which meant she wouldn't even have a minute to herself when she got home. He'd be there, right from the start. In her flat. Her tiny little flat. Alone with him.

'Kate, is something wrong?'

'Not a thing,' she said brightly. 'Everything's fine. Great. Terrific.'

Except that it wasn't, she thought as she followed him out of the hospital and into his car. In fact, she must have been insane to ever have agreed to him moving in with her.

Not insane, her mind whispered. Just desperate to get back to work at any price, and now she was going to have to pay that price. She was going to somehow have to forget what Mario looked like, forget how he made her feel when he smiled at her, and definitely get her libido under control. He was staying with her purely and simply for her own safety, so she had to pull herself together or there was a very real danger that she could end up looking like the biggest idiot of all time.

'So, that's it, then,' Kate said, all too aware that her voice had come out way too cheerleader bright but quite unable to prevent it. 'Now you know where everything is, you shouldn't get lost. Not that my flat is big enough to get lost in, of course…' Oh, sheesh, *shut up*, Kate. 'But if you ever did…'

'Forgive me for saying this,' Mario replied as he dumped his haversack in the middle of the sitting room. 'But why does virtually nothing in your home look as though you bought it?'

'Probably because I didn't,' she said. 'The people who owned this flat before me didn't want to take their furniture with them, so I sort of inherited it. I've been meaning to replace it, but…' She shrugged. 'I just haven't got round to it.'

'What you mean is, you don't want to buy anything to make this flat your home, because you don't feel as though it is.'

'You know, your ability to read my mind is getting seriously spooky,' she said with a nervous smile. 'I guess I've always felt sort of temporary here—as though there was no point in doing anything—but I will, eventually, of course.'

'You should live in the country,' he observed. 'In a grey granite house with little lattice windows, surrounded by an old-fashioned country garden.'

It sounded wonderful, but she shook her head.

'The commuting would be a nightmare, and you know the kind of hours I put in. I'd hardly ever be there.'

'Then work less hours,' he protested, 'learn to delegate. There's a whole world out there, Kate, and you're letting it pass you by.'

'I bet you work just as long hours as I do,' she protested and he smiled ruefully.

'Guilty, I'm afraid, but you really should think about moving out into the country. I can just picture you there, wearing one of those big straw hats, weeding in the garden—'

'News flash. I can't tell the difference between a weed and a flower,' she said, and he frowned at her.

'Look, whose fantasy is this?'

'You have a fantasy about me?' she said, beginning to laugh, but she stopped very fast when his eyes met hers then shot away, fast.

Oh, hell. Why had she said that? OK, so she hadn't meant it the way it had sounded, but she should never have said it. She should have said something casual, dismissive, innocuous, but, no. She had to go and suggest he had fantasies about her. Terrific, Kate. Really terrific.

'Would…?' She swallowed and started again. 'I know it's way past midnight, but would you like something to eat?'

'I don't want to be a nuisance—'

'You're not being a nuisance,' she insisted. 'I was going to have something myself, anyway, and there's some cold ham in the fridge with salad, or—'

'Cold ham sounds great,' he interrupted, looking every bit as uncomfortable as she felt until his glance fell on the copies of *La Bohème* and *Aida* sitting on top of her stereo. 'You lied about the heavy metal, Kate.'

'Which you knew,' she replied, without heat. 'So, I like opera, so what?'

'All those people singing at the top of their lungs, in a language most people don't understand.' He rolled his eyes. 'Give me Johnny Cash any day of the week.'

'I thought all Italians liked opera?' she said, and he gave her a hard stare.

'That's like saying all Scotsmen love the bagpipes, or all French people eat snails. It's a cliché.'

She laughed. 'I suppose so. I guess we'll just have to accept that we have completely opposite taste in music, although you know what they say about opp—' She came to a sudden halt, feeling her cheeks beginning to burn as she remembered, too late, what people actually said about opposites. 'I mean…what I meant was… What I intended to say was—'

'I think I might freshen up before dinner,' he interrupted, picking up his haversack. 'Get out of this uniform, if that's OK with you.'

'Oh, yes, definitely get out of your uniform!' she exclaimed, then bit her lip with mortification when she realised how suggestive that had sounded. 'I mean, you know where the bathroom is, so feel free to…to do whatever you want to do.'

And I want to die, she thought, when he walked out of the sitting room, and she sagged against the sofa.

What in the world was *wrong* with her? Half an hour—that was all the time he'd been in her flat—and every time she'd opened her mouth she'd managed to say something suggestive. He must think she was either a complete flake or coming on to him.

OK, when he came back from the bathroom she was going to stick to the weather, and the state of the NHS, she decided as she hurried into her kitchen and began pulling plates out of the cupboard. Nice, safe, boring topics that couldn't possibly result in her putting her foot in her mouth. In fact, it might be better if she didn't say anything at all. Just nodded, or shook her head, and gave up on conversation completely.

'Kate, what's this?'

'What's what?' she asked, taking the ham out of the fridge, and glancing over her shoulder, only to freeze, slack-jawed, when she saw that he had changed into his jeans.

The jeans she'd once thought scruffy, and yet now they looked sexy. Very sexy when they were teamed with a blue checked shirt that he hadn't bothered to button right up to the neck so she could see the deep V of olive skin at his throat. The throat she knew belonged to a broad muscular chest, a chest she'd been having X-rated dreams about for the past week.

'…your bathroom.'

'Sorry?' she said, dragging her gaze up from his throat to his blue eyes which were frowning. 'What did you say?'

'I *said*,' he declared, his eyes hardening as he held out a syringe to her, 'I found this in your bathroom.'

'It's…' She blinked and regrouped quickly. 'It's Anapen. I have an allergy to almonds so I always keep a supply in my bag, and in the bathroom.'

'Oh.'

A slight tinge of dark colour began to creep across his cheeks, and she stared at him in confusion, then the penny dropped.

'You thought I was taking drugs, didn't you?' she said, fighting down a smile.

'Suspicion goes with my job, Kate,' he said, looking more awkward than she'd ever seen him, and she took pity on him.

'The treatment for anaphylactic shock has moved on quite a bit since you were a doctor,' she said, taking the syringe from him. 'This isn't a normal syringe, it's an auto-injector. If I inadvertently eat some almonds, I just zap this into my thigh, and it immediately delivers a 0.3 milligram dose of adrenaline.'

He grimaced. 'Sounds painful.'

'It is, a bit,' she admitted, 'but it's better than the alternative— a full-blown anaphylactic attack.'

'How long have you had the allergy?' he asked curiously as she began heaping some salad onto two plates.

'Since I was seven. It's a bit of a nuisance because it means I can't eat out in restaurants. Just the tiniest trace of almond dust left on a spoon, and I go down like a stone.'

'That's scary,' he said with concern, and she shook her head.

'It's not a big deal, honestly.'

'Yes, but—'

'Mario, it *really* isn't a big deal, so relax, and eat, OK?' And, when he snapped into a smart salute, she shook her head at him. 'Oh, very funny. All right, I admit it. I'm bossy.'

'Not bossy,' he said as he sat down. 'You just won't be belittled, or put down, and those aren't bad attributes.'

'Perhaps not,' she said wryly. 'But they don't exactly win you friends.'

'And you want the kind of friends who would treat you like a doormat?' he said, and she looked at him, startled for a second, then her lips curved.

'I guess not, but I know I'm not easy to live with. My ex…' She picked up her knife and fork, then put them down again. 'He said I was my own worst enemy. That I was too driven, that I didn't always have to be a one woman crusader trying to change things, and…'

'You should remember you were married to him, and being his wife was the most important role in your life,' he finished for her, and she flushed.

'Something like that,' she admitted, and Mario shook his head.

'You married the wrong man, Kate.'

'Maybe. And you're not eating,' she said, deliberately changing the subject. 'I go to all the trouble of—'

'Putting some cold ham and salad on a plate,' he said, his eyes crinkling, and she laughed.

'OK, all right, so I didn't cook any of this, but eat, will you?' she said, and obediently he forked some salad into his mouth.

'Hey, this is good,' he declared.

'The local deli's finest,' she replied. 'What do you normally have for meals?'

'Takeaways,' he replied, and she shook her head at him.

'If that's what you normally live on then you're heading for clogged arteries and a coronary in a few years' time.'

'Probably.' He grinned. 'But I like living dangerously.'

Maybe that's what I ought to do, Kate thought as their eyes met. Ever since she was a little girl she'd had her three-point plan. To become an A and E consultant, to marry somebody who loved her and to have a nice home. Well, she'd struck out on two of those things, so maybe she ought to give up on plans, throw caution to the winds and live dangerously for a while. Just a little while.

'Kate…?'

'You're…you're not eating,' she said through a throat that was suddenly far too tight.

'Neither are you.'

His voice was husky, sending tiny shivers up the back of her spine and, as his eyes held hers, deep and blue and liquid, she felt her blood heat up, and her breath go. Oh, lord, but she wanted this man. Wanted him to hold her, to kiss her, to make love to her.

Lust, her mind whispered, and she bit her lip, and saw Mario's eyes darken. She didn't give a damn if it was lust. She didn't give a damn about anything. She just wanted him to make love to her. Now.

'Kate…'

She leant towards him, and he leant forwards, too, and then suddenly he stood up, his cheeks slightly flushed.

'I… You were right,' he muttered. 'It *is* late, so maybe I should just turn in.'

'Oh, right,' she said. 'The sofa—it's actually a sofa bed. I don't know how comfortable it will be—'

'I can sleep anywhere.'

His voice was brusque, dismissive, and she forced a bright and perky smile to her lips as she got to her feet, too.

'Do you want me to help you make up the bed? There's a spare duvet in the hall cupboard, and sheets—'

'I can manage, thanks.'

'Right. Good.' Oh, hell, but how could she have been so crass, so stupid, so downright *obvious*? He was edging towards the kitchen door, not meeting her eyes, clearly as embarrassed as hell, and her cheeks were red, and she hated the fact that they were red. 'I'll... I'll see you in the morning, then,' she said.

'OK,' he muttered.

He also muttered something else, but she didn't catch what it was, couldn't have, not at the speed he was moving.

Don't think about it, she told herself, as she limply sat down again at the kitchen table. Forget about it. Pretend it never happened. Pretend you didn't lean towards him, clearly inviting him to kiss you. Pretend you didn't say all those dumb, obvious things, but all the pretending in the world wouldn't have worked.

'Oh, damn,' she said, as she put her head down on the kitchen table with a groan. 'Damn, damn, *damn*.'

CHAPTER SIX

'HELL, mate, but you look rough this evening,' Ralph Evanton declared as he and Mario stood in Kate's office. 'Bad shift?'

Bad shift, bad week, Mario thought, but he didn't say that.

'What have you got for me?' he said instead. 'And can you make it quick? It's bedlam in the treatment room and I don't want to be away for too long.'

'That won't be a problem because there's precious little to tell,' Ralph replied. 'Faranelli and Di Angelis boarded a plane this morning to New York which means they're either worried we might be getting closer to them or—as is more likely—their wives fancy doing a bit of shopping in the Big Apple.'

'And Mackay?' Mario asked.

'In Glasgow for his daughter's wedding.'

Which meant the big three knew they were getting no closer to nailing them, Mario thought with a sigh, and the longer they got nowhere the less likely it was that they would ever get a conviction.

'Alert the NYPD that Faranelli and Di Angelis are on their patch, and keep the tail on Mackay. Apart from that...' Mario shook his head. 'We wait. That's all we can do.'

Ralph nodded, and slipped his notebook back into his pocket.

'It's a pity Kate has never been able to remember the other

name that Hamilton gave her,' he observed. 'It might have been of someone lower down the chain—someone easier for us to nail.'

'All she can remember is that it was the name of a town,' Mario replied, rubbing his fingers wearily over his face. 'Which isn't exactly helpful.'

'No. So, how's it going, living with Kate?'

'I am not living with Kate,' Mario replied, trying and failing to keep the edge out of his voice. 'I have simply moved in with her to protect her.'

'Yes, but how's it going?' Ralph pressed, and Mario shot him a glance of irritation.

'Fine,' he said.

But it wasn't fine, Mario thought, as he walked slowly back to the treatment room. In fact, he could safely say that the past week had been one of the worst weeks of his life. *Dio*, but he couldn't believe even now that he'd actually admitted to Kate that he had fantasies about her. OK, so at least he hadn't confessed to the one where she was naked in his bed, and he was sliding hard into her round wet softness, but he should never have admitted to having *any* sort of fantasy about her.

'Suspected hip fracture in cubicle 1,' Terri declared the minute she saw him. 'Eighty-two-year-old white female, name Eleanor Wallace, in a lot of pain but otherwise bright as a button. She tripped over in the street, and was brought in by ambulance about an hour and a half ago.'

'An hour and a—'

'No need to leap up onto your soap box, Mario,' Terri interrupted with a smile, seeing his expression. 'Kate asked for both AP pelvis and lateral hip X-rays so we shipped Mrs Wallace along to X-Ray, and this is her just back. Kate will be here in a couple of minutes, so could you take some blood samples from Mrs Wallace for glucose, FBC, and U and E?'

In other words, he was going to be working with Kate again, Mario thought with a sinking heart.

But that was what you wanted, his mind pointed out, to work alongside her, to make sure she was safe.

Yes, but that was before I was spending twenty-four hours a day with her, he argued back. Twenty-four nerve-jangling, libido inflammatory hours.

'Mario?'

Terri was gazing at him expectantly and he nodded.

'Blood samples. Got it. What about her IV line?'

'I've just checked it, and it's running smoothly with no sign of her developing shock.'

'Won't she also need an ECG reading to rule out the possibility of arrhythmias or MI?' Mario said quickly as the sister turned to go, and she grinned at him.

'Of course she will, but I knew I didn't need to tell you that,' she said and, with a wink, she sped off, leaving him gazing after her in confusion.

Terri had been winking a lot at him recently, and it wasn't that he objected to a woman winking at him but it was…weird. As though the sister knew something he didn't, and if he'd learned one thing during his eight years in the police force it was that being kept in the dark was bad news.

'I thought that nice young lady doctor was coming back to see me?' Mrs Wallace said when he opened the curtains around cubicle 1. 'The one with the lovely hair.'

'Dr Kennedy,' Mario declared. 'She'll be along in a minute with the results of your X-rays, but first I need to take some blood samples from you, and link you to this little monitor to check your heart.'

'Don't nurses usually do that sort of thing?' Mrs Wallace observed as she watched Mario place some adhesive suckers on her chest, then collect an array of sample bottles from the instrument trolley.

'I am a nurse,' Mario said, and waited for the snarky comment or disparaging observation that usually greeted his words, but to his surprise the elderly lady beamed up at him.

'Good for you, Nurse…' She peered at his name tag. 'Nurse Volante. It's way past time there were more male nurses in the profession, particularly…' Her faded brown eyes twinkled. '…when they're such very good-looking ones.'

'Why, Mrs Wallace, I do believe you're flirting with me.' He laughed, and she dimpled up at him.

'You know something, Nurse Volante,' she said. 'I do believe you're right.'

He laughed again, and he was still laughing when Kate stepped through the curtains.

'Sounds like somebody's having a good time,' she said, and Mrs Wallace nodded.

'I'm thinking of tripping over every week from now on!' the elderly woman exclaimed. 'Meeting this handsome young man has been a real tonic.'

'Well, he's certainly different,' Kate said lightly as she squeezed past Mario to clip Mrs Wallace's X-rays up onto the display panel.

Dio mio, but did these damn cubicles have to be quite so small? Mario thought, sucking in his breath sharply as he felt Kate's hip brush the top of his thigh. It was bad enough living with her in such a small flat without her invading his work space, too.

Not that he believed for one moment that Kate was deliberately crowding him. In fact, ever since he'd moved into her flat, it had been quite the opposite. Whenever his gaze met hers she seemed to find something else incredibly interesting. If he appeared in the sitting room or the kitchen she immediately found a pressing reason to be somewhere else. It was almost as though she sensed what he was thinking, and he hoped to heaven she didn't. Not when most of his thoughts consisted of an over-whelming desire to drag her into his arms and make love to her until they were both senseless.

'It looks like a Garden 11 to me,' Kate murmured as she flicked the switch on the display monitor then moved from plate to plate. 'It's not obvious in this one,' she continued, pointing to the X-ray, 'but if you look at numbers 4 and 5 you can just see a fracture line from the superior to inferior cortex.'

'Yes,' he muttered.

'I don't think there's anything else,' she said, scanning the plates intently. 'What do you think?'

Twelve feet, he thought as she tilted her head and her perfume filled his senses. Twelve feet was all that separated them both when they went to bed at night, him on his narrow sofa bed, and her in her big, roomy double bed, and he knew it was a big, roomy double bed because he'd seen it one morning when she'd forgotten to shut her bedroom door. Twelve tiny little feet between him and all her lush roundness, and he knew he was going to go crazy if he didn't have her soon, just as he also knew that he couldn't have her. Mustn't. Not ever.

'Mario,' she repeated, a slight frown creasing her forehead. 'I said, what do you think?'

That I'm going insane, he thought. That I'm losing it com-pletely, and if I don't somehow regain control of my rampant libido I'm going to do something really, *really* stupid.

'I don't see anything else either,' he forced himself to reply, and Kate turned back to Mrs Wallace with a regretful smile.

'I'm afraid you've definitely fractured your hip, Mrs Wallace,' she declared. 'It's not a bad fracture, but it's not some-thing I can treat. I'll arrange for you to be transferred to Orthopaedics—'

'You mean, I'm going to have to stay in hospital?' the elderly woman exclaimed with clear dismay. 'But what about my dog—Trixie? There's only me to look after her.'

'Haven't you any relatives we can phone?' Kate suggested. 'Or a neighbour who might be prepared to look after Trixie for you?'

'My son's on holiday in France and he won't be back for a fortnight,' Mrs Wallace replied, 'and I wouldn't let my next door neighbour look after a stick insect. The man's an idiot.'

'Perhaps the RSPCA might be able to help?' Mario suggested. 'If it's only for a fortnight until your son returns…?'

Mrs Wallace shook her head violently.

'The RSPCA will put her in a kennel, and Trixie—she's family, and you don't put family in a kennel. No, I'm sorry, but we'll just have to forget about the hip. It's not that painful—honestly it isn't.'

'Mrs Wallace, you can't leave,' Kate insisted with dismay, as the elderly lady attempted to sit up, only to suddenly become very white in the face. 'That hip won't heal on its own, and if you don't have treatment you'll end up in a wheelchair.'

'Yes, but you don't understand, Doctor,' the elderly lady declared, tears flooding her eyes. 'Trixie… My husband bought her for me as a birthday present when she was just a puppy. She's all I have left of him since he died four years ago, and to put her in a kennel… What if anything happened to her—what if she pined away before my son came back from France?'

Kate gazed impotently at Mario, and he cleared his throat.

'Mrs Wallace, would you let Dr Kennedy transfer you to Orthopaedics if I arranged for a friend of mine to look after your dog?'

The elderly lady gazed back at him uncertainly. 'Is he trustworthy, this friend of yours?'

'He's in the police force,' Mario declared, 'and I don't think you can get more trustworthy than that, do you?'

'Well, in that case—if you're sure it can be arranged…?' Mrs Wallace said hesitantly, and Mario smiled at her.

'Consider it done,' he said, but after Mrs Wallace had been transferred to the orthopaedics ward Kate turned to him with a half smile.

'Do you often volunteer friends for dog-sitting duties without asking them first?'

'Tom won't mind,' Mario replied. 'He loves dogs, and so does his wife. They'll be more than happy to oblige.'

'Really?' she said, her smile widening, and he looked embarrassed.

'Let's just say he owes me a favour, and I'm collecting.'

'You know, you really are a big softie under that tough exterior, aren't you?' She laughed, but he didn't.

In fact, he backed up a step.

'Is it OK, if I use the unit phone to call Tom?' he said. 'I'd better give him Mrs Wallace's address and tell him to pick up her dog.'

'Of course it's OK!' she exclaimed, but she heaved a heavy sigh when he sped down the treatment room without as much as a backward glance.

A week. Mario had only been living with her for a week and it had been—without doubt—the worst week of her life. Not that he had done anything to induce the lustful, lascivious thoughts that kept plaguing both her waking and her sleeping hours. In fact, he'd behaved like a perfect gentleman. Not crowding her, keeping everything light and casual, and she was the one who was continually flustered, the one who kept inventing reasons to get away from him, and it was driving her crazy.

Look, when are you going to wake up and face reality? her mind whispered. He's not interested. OK, so he flirted with you before he moved into your home but he's half Italian, for God's sake, and Italian men can't resist chatting up women—all women. And if he was looking for a relationship it would be with a twenty-two-year-old, size 4 model, whereas you... You're an overweight, workaholic, cranky woman with attitude who will be thirty-five in a week so why in the world would he ever be interested in you?

George was, she thought as she reached for the whiteboard eraser and saw the replacement porter watching her from outside cubicle 6. In fact, if she was honest, she was beginning to find his constant scrutiny unnerving. So unnerving that she'd actually seriously considered telling Mario about it, but what would she say?

'The new porter keeps staring at me.'

It sounded so wimpy, so pathetic.

So was Paul, she thought with irritation, as the specialist registrar strode past her without a word.

'He loved ruling the roost when you were off sick.' Terri laughed when she'd talked to her about him. 'And now you've come back, and taken all his power away. No wonder he's put you in the dog house.'

Maybe that's what she ought to do, Kate thought, as she saw Terri answering their emergency phone, and knew that an ambulance was on its way. Buy a dog, and give up on trying to understand men completely.

'Burns victim on the way,' Terri exclaimed. 'ETA five minutes.'

Kate nodded, but her heart sank. If there was one thing she hated it was burns cases. It was the look, and the sickly sweet smell, she couldn't stand, had never been able to.

Please let another case come in first, she prayed. Please let Paul have to deal with the burns case, and I get an accidental poisoning or another fractured leg, but of course she didn't.

As though on cue, the door of the treatment room banged open and two paramedics appeared.

'Burns case, Doc,' one of the paramedics announced. 'Homeless guy who seems to have fallen asleep in the park while drinking and smoking, and set himself alight. A passing bus driver called it.'

'Do we know his name, his age?' she asked, trying hard not

to breathe in too deeply as Mario helped the paramedics lever the man onto the examination trolley.

'No ID, Doc, and as for his age—your guess is as good as mine,' the paramedic replied. 'He could be anywhere between fifty and seventy. Living rough ages them fast.'

It did, Kate thought, as she stared down at the man and tried not to shudder, but, dear lord, he was a mess. His hair had melted to his head, his face and tongue were grotesquely swollen and he had no eyebrows left at all.

'Terri, cut off the remainder of his clothes and insert a Foley catheter before his penis closes up completely,' she said as the sister joined them. 'Mario, keep a watch on his oxygen levels, renew his Haemaccel drip or he'll go into shock for sure, and get me a BP and pulse. We'll also need blood samples for cross-matching.'

'IV of titrated morphine, too?' Terri added as she reached for the scissors, and Kate nodded.

If the rest of the homeless man's injuries were as bad as his face then all they could do was to try to stabilise his condition. It would be the burns unit who would have the job of repairing the damage to his skin but first they had to make sure he lived long enough to be transferred there.

'Do you have a BP and pulse reading yet?' she asked after Mario had held a Doppler probe over the man's carotid area because there wasn't enough skin left on the man's wrist or throat to get a reading.

'BP 90 over 70, cardiac output down thirty per cent,' he replied. 'Pulse 130 and rising.'

It wasn't good, it wasn't good at all, and when Terri had removed all of the man's clothing Kate had to bite down hard on her lip to prevent uttering an exclamation of horror. If she'd thought the injuries to his face and head were bad, it was as nothing compared to his body. His arms and legs were blackened like burnt sticks and so, too, were his buttocks and chest.

'Thank God he's unconscious,' Terri murmured, and Kate agreed with her.

When skin burned it shrank just like a sausage skin did after you'd put it onto a barbecue, but the difference between a sausage skin and human skin was that when human skin shrank the muscle beneath the skin became compressed, cutting off the blood supply. If the muscles didn't get blood they would die, which meant there was only one thing Kate could do.

'Scalpel,' she said, and Mario's eyes met hers.

Had he hated doing this as much as she did when he was a doctor? she wondered. Maybe he hadn't. A lot of doctors performed the procedure without a second's thought, but it always made her feel slightly sick even though she knew she had to free the tissue as quickly as possible and this was the only way to do it.

Squaring her shoulders, she took the scalpel from Mario's outstretched hand, and quickly began making long thin cuts across the homeless man's chest, arms, and hands. Almost immediately, the muscles began popping through the slashes showing that their blood supply was moving again, and that they at least would live.

'I don't think I'm ever going to eat another barbecued sausage again,' Mario murmured as he watched the muscles appear, and Kate managed a shaky laugh.

'I haven't eaten one since the first time I did this procedure,' she admitted.

'BP still falling,' Terry declared, 'and look at his catheter.'

It was filling with dark urine which meant that the homeless man had either a stomach or bowel blockage due to smoke inhalation, and unless that was treated quickly he would die.

'Page OR and tell them we've got an urgent one,' Kate said.

Within seconds the homeless man was being wheeled towards the operating theatre and, as Terri set off to assist Paul, Kate wearily peeled off her latex gloves and tossed them into the bin.

'It's not looking good for him, is it?' Mario said.

'With those burns, and a blockage…' Kate shook her head. 'If he makes it, it will be a miracle but then the OR people often do perform miracles.'

'I always liked them when I was a doctor,' Mario observed. 'Not big on humour, and woe betide you if you went into their operating theatre without scrubs, but they were a great bunch of guys.'

'Guys?' Kate repeated, shooting him a pointed sidelong glance, and he grinned.

'There weren't any female OR consultants in my time.'

'Still aren't many even now,' Kate said, and Mario stared at her thoughtfully for a moment, then cleared his throat.

'When I was a doctor, what I hated most was people being sick. I could take any amount of blood or sputum, even the most horrific of burns, but if someone was sick I suddenly discovered a very pressing need to check their X-rays.'

'Was it that obvious?' she said uncomfortably. 'That I hate burns cases?'

'Only to me,' he said, his lips curving into a gentle smile, 'but then I reckon I'm getting to know what's going on in your mind pretty well.'

She hoped he wasn't, because what she wanted most right now was to walk straight into his arms, and be held by him. To forget just for one moment that she was the A and E consultant, and to simply be a woman who needed to be hugged and comforted.

'Kate…?'

His eyes were fixed on her and she heard the sound of a distant siren.

'I think it's going to be one of those nights,' she said.

It was.

By eleven o'clock the treatment room looked like a war zone, and by midnight as though a bloodbath had occurred. They'd had four MVAs in quick succession, and they'd lost them all.

Four young drivers who were never going to see their twenty-first birthdays. Four young men who ought to have just been starting out in life, but this was as far along in life as they were going to get.

'It's time to go home, Kate,' Mario said, coming to stand beside her as the night staff began to arrive and she leant against the treatment room wall, her eyes closed with exhaustion, her shoulders slumped.

'I know,' she murmured. 'I just have to do something first.'

'Kate—'

'I only want to phone the burns unit,' she interrupted, seeing his forehead furrow. 'To find out how the homeless man is doing.'

'OK, but make it fast,' he replied. 'You look all in.'

She felt it, too, when the burns unit confirmed what she had already suspected. That the homeless man hadn't made it to them, but had died on the operating table.

'You can't win them all, Kate,' Mario said as he accompanied her out of the hospital towards his car, and she gazed heavenwards impotently.

'I know, but sometimes it's just so unnecessary!' she exclaimed. 'Take those young men. If they had just been wearing seat belts, had been driving a little slower, not been drinking before they got into their cars, they'd all have been up in Men's Surgical right now instead of in the morgue. *Why* can't people learn? What will it take before they realise that a car is a death trap if you get into it drunk, or drive it too fast without a seat belt?'

'I don't know,' Mario replied as he opened the car door for her, but when she slipped into the passenger seat he said, 'Look, why don't I take care of dinner tonight?'

A small smile tugged at the corner of her mouth. 'From the man who normally lives on takeaways, this should be good. What did you have in mind?'

'How about chicken biryani, or pizza?'

'You know how to cook those?' she said, impressed, and his lips curved.

'No, but I do know the best takeaway in Aberdeen. Come on, Kate,' he added as she shook her head at him. 'Think of the plusses. We get great food, and no washing-up. Not even the knives and forks because they throw in those little plastic ones for free.'

It sounded stodgy, and fattening, and terrific.

'OK, make mine a pizza,' she said. 'Pepperoni, with noodles on the side.'

'You want noodles with pizza?' he said, his expression showing what he thought of that combination, and she nodded.

'Yes, I want noodles.'

'OK. Whatever you want tonight, you get.'

She wished that was true when he stopped at the takeaway and she sat in the car, watching the raindrops slide slowly down the car windscreen. She wished even more that he could produce a magic wand and wave away the hollow, empty feeling she felt inside her this evening, but he couldn't. Nobody could. Not when she couldn't forget the four young men who would never see another dawn, and the homeless man—especially the homeless man—who had died on the operating table without anybody knowing his name.

'What say we just pull the coffee table over to the sofa, and eat there?' Mario asked when they got back to her flat. 'Forget about the kitchen table for tonight?'

'Sounds good to me,' she replied, dropping her handbag on the sideboard and slipping off her shoes.

'I bought some wine, too,' he continued as he disappeared into the kitchen, and she heard the clink of glasses. 'I didn't know what kind you liked so I bought both red and white.'

'White would be great,' she said, sitting down on the sofa and closing her eyes.

Lord, but she was tired, so tired. She felt as though she could sleep for a week, but she knew the minute she went to bed she would start reliving the events of the evening, and when morning came she'd be lucky if she'd managed to grab even half an hour of sleep.

'Your wine and food, my lady,' Mario declared, and she opened her eyes to see he'd pulled the coffee table over to the sofa, opened the styrofoam containers, and poured them each a glass of wine. 'Eat, drink and enjoy.'

'It certainly smells good,' she said, sitting up and breaking off a piece of the pizza. 'Tastes good, too,' she added as she put the piece in her mouth and savoured it.

'I told you I knew the best takeaway in Aberdeen.'

'So you did.'

He sat down beside her, and fixed her with a penetrating stare. 'OK, when you're as quiet as this I know something's wrong, so give.'

'I'm just tired,' she said and he put down his pizza.

'Kate, I've seen you put in a sixteen-hour day, and still be running on all cylinders,' he declared. 'Talk to me. Tell me.'

She took a forkful of noodles. 'Hey, now these really *are* good.'

'Quit stalling, Kennedy,' he said, his voice mock stern. 'Tell me what's bothering you.'

'It's…' She bit her lip. 'That homeless man, Mario. It's not just that he was so horrifically burned, and I hate burns, it's… Why do some people end up in the back of an alley, or on a park bench, homeless and unloved, with nobody to mourn them?'

'According to the experts, each and every one of us is only three pay cheques away from the gutter,' he observed, and she shook her head as she sipped her wine.

'I know that's what they say, but do you think there's ever a moment when we do something, or something is done to us, and that thing—whatever it is—suddenly changes our future for ever and instead of having families, and friends, and homes, we end up with a life of misery and loneliness?'

'The road not taken, you mean,' he murmured, 'or perhaps the road we choose to take without fully realising where it will lead?'

'Something like that.' She nodded, and his expression saddened.

'Yes, I think there can be such a moment. I wish I didn't believe it, but I do.'

He was speaking from personal experience, she knew he was, and she wished she dared ask what had happened but his closed face didn't encourage her to probe.

'How do you cope in your work?' she said tentatively instead. 'You must have seen some pretty horrendous things during your time with the police force. How do you deal with it, live with it?'

'The same way you do,' he said, swallowing some of his pizza then letting his head fall back next to hers against the back of the sofa. 'By developing a certain detachment from the emotional aspects of a case. If I didn't, I wouldn't be able to concentrate on doing my job properly. This isn't to say, of course, that there aren't some cases that get to me more than others.'

Like kids, and teenagers, she thought.

'You're not just trying to prove you're as good as the cop who came up through the ranks, are you?' she said. 'You honestly want to make the world a better place.'

'So do you,' he declared. 'Being a consultant isn't an ego trip for you. You care about your patients, want the best for them, and if that means standing on people's toes you'll do it.'

'In other words, I'm bossy,' she said, and he frowned at her.

'Haven't we had this conversation before? Yes, you have strong opinions, but you're also honest and caring, and straight as a die, Kate, so don't ever change. You're great just the way you are, and the world needs people like you.'

And that, she suddenly realised as she stared back at him, was why she liked him so much. He didn't want her to change. He didn't want her to compromise what she believed in, to make adjustments, to be less driven, or even less bossy than she knew she could be. He liked her just the way she was, faults and all.

But he was going to leave. When his investigation was over, or if he discovered he couldn't make a case out of what happened to Duncan Hamilton, he would leave, and she'd never see him again, and she didn't want to never see him again.

'Would you ever consider going back into medicine?' she said quickly. 'My department needs somebody like you.' *I need you. You make me laugh, you make me feel good about myself, and I don't want you to go.* 'If you updated your skills—'

'I love what I do now, Kate,' he interrupted. 'For you, medicine is the best job in the world, but for me, it's the police force. Actually, when I think about it,' he continued with a slight frown as he took another bite of his pizza, 'our jobs aren't that dissimilar. And you're not eating,' he added. 'I go to all the trouble of buying you that insult to Italian cuisine, so the least you can do is eat it.'

'I'm eating—I'm eating!' she exclaimed, forking some of the noodles into her mouth. 'How are our jobs similar?'

'You want to cure individuals, I want to cure society. We're both crusaders.' A grin tugged at his lips. 'I'm just incredibly relieved I don't have to wear the cape and tights.'

'*You're* relieved?' she exclaimed. 'I bet you'd look like an Italian god in a cape and tights, whereas I'd look like a munchkin.' He let out a snort of laughter, then coughed as a piece of his pizza went down the wrong way, and she slapped him on the back. 'Hey, don't choke on me. I'm off duty, remember, and I'm not really up for the kiss of life tonight.'

'No?' he said, his eyes meeting hers, and her own breath caught and lodged in her throat.

Don't read any more into that than there actually is, she told herself, feeling her heart begin to race. Don't make a fool of yourself by saying something dumb the way you always seem to when he's around, but she didn't get a chance to say anything.

'I'm sorry,' Mario said quickly, a rich tide of colour staining his cheeks. 'I shouldn't have said that, and I apologise. I'm supposed to be here to protect you, not to take advantage of you.'

He looked embarrassed, and uncomfortable, and she knew she ought to smile, and nod, and say something casual and flippant, but she didn't want to be casual, flippant. She wanted him. She wanted him so much it was a physical ache.

'Mario, what if…?' She could feel her cheeks beginning to redden, hear her voice shaking slightly, and took a steadying breath. *Dammit, Kate, just say it, and to hell with the consequences.* 'What if I said I wanted you to take advantage of me?'

His eyes shot to hers and she saw something dark and hot stir in them then it was gone.

'If you said that I'd say you needed your head examined,' he declared, his mouth tight, as he reached for his glass of wine.

'Well, in that case, you'd better book me an appointment tomorrow with the hospital psychiatrist,' she said softly, 'because I do want you, Mario Volante. I think I've wanted you from the very first moment we met.'

His hand stilled over his glass of wine, and he turned to face her, his expression bleak.

'Kate, you don't know what you're saying.'

'So, I'm stupid now—is that it?' she said, and he shook his head impatiently.

'Of course you're not, but, I don't do commitment, Kate, I don't do long term. My wife…' His lips twisted. 'Do you know how long Sue and I were married? Eighteen months. Just eighteen months and I'm amazed she stayed with me that long.'

'You mean you cheated on her?' she said, not wanting to believe it, but needing to know.

He closed his eyes, and his voice when he spoke was desolate.

'Yes, I cheated on her but not in the way you think. I cheated because I married her knowing I didn't love her, knowing I still loved somebody else.'

'The…the somebody else,' Kate said awkwardly. 'Was it— is it—the girl in the photograph—the photograph you carry in your wallet?'

He nodded. 'Her name was Antonia, and she died two years before Sue and I met.'

And you still love her, Kate thought with an unaccountable stab of pain, or why else do you still keep her photograph in your wallet?

'Then why did you marry Sue?' she asked with more edge than she'd intended. 'Surely it was a cruel thing to do, to marry somebody you knew you didn't love?'

'Don't you think I haven't told myself that over and over again since we divorced?' he said harshly. 'But I thought—hoped—that I might grow to love her. She was so kind, you see, so generous, and I…' He swallowed. 'I was hurting pretty badly at the time, and I wanted—I really did want—it to work, but it didn't.'

She stared into his deep blue eyes, saw the pain and heartache there, but she also saw a raw need, a need she felt herself, and she reached out and clasped his hands in hers.

'Mario, I don't care what you did in the past!' she exclaimed, willing him to believe her, 'and I'm not asking you for any sort of commitment. I just want you. Even if it's only for tonight, I want you.'

'You say that now,' he murmured, 'but what about when you wake up with me tomorrow and realise you've made a terrible mistake? And it would be a mistake, Kate,' he added, his face bleak, 'because I can't offer you anything. The caring part of me, the loving part, died with Antonia.'

'Mario, didn't you hear what I said? I'm not expecting or looking for commitment. Hell's bells, I only just got divorced so the last thing I'm looking for is a long-term relationship. I'm a single, unattached woman of sound mind—'

'That's highly debatable.'

'Who will be thirty-five next week,' she continued, 'and I can't see what would be so very wrong in us making love if we both accept and agree that there would be no strings attached.'

'Kate, it wouldn't be wrong for me, but for you…' He shook his head. 'Women see things differently. For them, making love isn't a casual act they can immediately forget. It means more to them. It involves putting their hearts on the line.'

'Not any more it doesn't,' she protested. 'This is the twenty-first century, Mario. Women can have casual flings, and then walk away with no hard feelings on either side.'

Well, at least that's what she'd heard modern women did. She'd never done it herself, but maybe she should have. Maybe that was what had been wrong with her life up until now. She had never simply acted on instinct, and she should have done.

'*Dio*, Kate, maybe some women can do that!' he exclaimed. 'But you… You're different, and you sure as hell are worth more than a casual fling. You're bright, and funny, and caring, and—'

'OK, let's cut to the chase,' she interrupted, letting go of his hands though her heart ached at the unhappiness she could see in his face. 'What you're really saying is *you* don't want to wake up tomorrow, and think, dear lord, how did I end up in bed with such a fat woman?'

'Kate, you are *not* fat!' he exclaimed. 'You are a lush, gorgeous, sexy woman, and I want to make love to you, but…'

'So are you trying to tell me—very subtly, of course—that you're lousy in bed?' she said. 'That I'm going to be disappointed?'

His mouth fell open, then a glimmer of a smile appeared on his lips.

'It's not going to work, Kate. You are not going to make me angry, and, yes, I'm lousy in bed.'

'Prove it,' she said, and his smile widened for a moment then disappeared.

'Kate, listen—'

'No, *you* listen,' she interrupted. 'I know we don't love one another but I do know we're attracted to one another, and for me that's enough. Dammit, if you'd brought any of your Johnny Cash CDs with you I'd even be prepared to let you play them at full blast to prove that I mean what I say.'

'And greater sacrifice can no opera loving woman make,' he said, his lips creasing into a reluctant grin. 'But, Kate—'

'Mario, I know what I'm doing!' she exclaimed. 'Just as I also know that you're lonely and unhappy, and I...' Her voice broke. 'I'm lonely, and unhappy, too, and maybe... Maybe we can help each other, comfort each other, take away the loneliness and the unhappiness just for a little while.'

She could see the indecision in his face, the heartbreak, the desire, and then, just when she thought it was hopeless, that she was going to be sleeping alone in her big double bed again, he suddenly reached for her.

'Oh, *Dio*, Kate,' he said savagely. *'Li desidera, anche.'*

And his lips met hers and took her breath away.

'What you just said?' she gasped when she surfaced for air. 'Was that good?'

'Yes, it was good,' he said, kissing her again, and this time his tongue met hers, hot and devastating, and she arched against him, feeling her blood surge, and her heart race, and she held onto him, never wanting to let him go.

'I'm going to have to take Italian lessons,' she said breathlessly when he trailed a searing row of kisses across her lips, her cheeks, her throat. 'So I'll know when you're lying to me.'

'I won't ever lie to you,' he said, his voice ragged. 'You might not always like what I say, but I won't ever lie to you.'

'I don't care if you lie, I just... Oh, *God*, that feels so...so...'

She bit her lip and convulsed as he slipped his hand under her blouse and she felt his fingers hot on her breast.

'Good?' he whispered into her neck, as he eased his fingers inside her bra and slowly began to tease her nipple with his thumb.

'Yes—oh, *yes*,' she said, feeling a heat beginning to flare deep and low in the pit of her stomach. 'Just don't stop. Please, don't stop.'

He didn't. He lowered her back onto the sofa, trapping her beneath him, and very soon her clothes were gone, and so were his.

'Kate, oh, *Dio*, Kate,' he said thickly as his fingers found the pulsing slippery rush between her thighs, and he began to stroke her, gently at first and then more insistently, but though she squirmed with pleasure it wasn't enough, she wanted more, much more.

Quickly she rolled on top of him, and he gasped and shuddered as she began to lick her way down his chest, but when she cupped him with her fingers, he caught her wrist to stay her.

'Kate, this is madness,' he said with difficulty. 'We shouldn't—I shouldn't…'

'I don't care,' she said, every nerve ending inside her screaming for release. '*I don't care.*'

And he rolled her back under him again, and kissed her, touching her everywhere with his hands and his lips, and just when she thought she wouldn't be able to bear any more he suddenly slid inside her, hard and slick and deep, and she sucked in her breath and clutched him to her, no longer knowing where she began or he did.

'Kate, oh *sei belissima*,' he groaned as he pulled back, making her moan and gasp with longing, and then he drove deeper, rocking harder and harder into her, and she felt his arms shake as he balanced his weight on them, and rose up to meet him, catching his rhythm, so that the heat began to build, deep and low, leaving her weak with pleasure and wanting.

Frantically, she dug her fingernails into his back, and called his name, urging him on, feeling the pressure tightening deep inside her, knowing she was almost there, almost there. She could feel it coming, feel herself beginning to fall over the edge, and suddenly she gasped and convulsed, and began spiralling and spiralling and spasming over and over again. And then, while she was still holding onto him, still shuddering from the shattering ecstasy, he convulsed, too, and collapsed into her arms.

'You…you lied,' she said, when her thundering heart finally allowed her to speak.

'About what?' he said, looking exhausted as he lifted his head to gaze at her.

'About being lousy in bed.'

He grinned.

'I know,' he said, and she punched him lightly on the shoulder.

'Macho Italian show-off,' she said, trying not to smile and failing miserably.

'You're no slouch in bed yourself,' he said, kissing her lightly. 'In fact, you're phenomenal.'

And she laughed, but as he rolled onto his back and gathered her against his chest she didn't tell him that it had never been quite like this for her before. Not with her ex-husband, not with anyone. It had been her best sex, ever.

And that was all it had been, she reminded herself, as she felt him kiss the top of her head. She'd gone into this with no illusions—hell, she'd been the one who had talked him into making love with her—so she was going to simply enjoy it while it lasted and when they parted she'd smile and wish him well. Modern women did it all the time so she could, too.

Couldn't she?

CHAPTER SEVEN

A SLOW smile curved Kate's lips as she stared down the unit and saw Mario smile back. They'd been lovers now for a week, and it amazed her that they'd both once had doubts. Even this morning when he'd pressed a small, wrapped box into her hand, and muttered an awkward, 'Happy Birthday,' she'd been able to accept the gift for what it was and not for one second seen it as any kind of token of intent.

Yes, it was working out perfectly, she told herself, as Mario began to walk towards her, his blue eyes dancing. Modern women didn't need—or expect—to hear the 'L' word. They just took their pleasure where they found it, and that was what she was doing, and it was working.

'How's my birthday girl?'

'Good,' she replied, her hand going automatically to her throat where she could feel the small heart-shaped pendant he had given her nestling against her skin.

'And it's going to get even better,' he murmured huskily into her ear. 'Tonight, after dinner, wonderful things are going to happen to you.'

They already had, she thought, feeling her heart kick up at the heat in his eyes, but no way was she ever going to admit it. It wouldn't be cool or modern, and she was determined to be cool and modern, so she murmured back, 'Promises, promises,' and saw him grin.

'Anybody ever tell you you're asking for trouble, Kate Kennedy?'

'You have,' she said, trying not to smile. 'More times than I care to remember.'

'It obviously hasn't sunk in, though, has it?' he observed. 'In fact, I think I'm going to have to take you in hand.'

'Now, that sounds promising,' she said, her cheeks dimpling. 'What have you got in mind? Handcuffs—padlocks—a little—'

'Well, this is a great start to the day!' Terri exclaimed, striding towards them, her face tight. 'Colin's going to be late because his car won't start, two of my nurses have phoned in sick and, in case you've both forgotten, Paul is going to his cousin's wedding this afternoon so we'll be without him as well.'

'Right,' Kate replied, glaring hard at Mario, daring him to say anything. 'Have you phoned the nursing agency to see if they can supply us with anybody?'

'Well, shucks, no,' Terri declared waspishly. 'I thought it might be fun to see how we could manage without two nurses. *Of course* I've phoned the agency but they can't get us anyone until noon so we're presumably supposed to put a sign on the unit door saying, *If you're critically ill, please come back later.*'

'Terri—'

'And Admin have been on the phone saying they haven't received the referral notes for that mushroom poisoning case and of course Paul is blaming me, saying I must've lost them and…and…' Tears welled in the sister's eyes. 'I shouldn't take this out on you, Kate, but I really don't need it, I don't.'

'You know, I think I might just see if anybody needs me,' Mario declared, edging his way down the treatment room, with a look on his face that said, *Oh, hell, crying woman, I'm out of here,* and Kate scowled back at him with an answering gaze of, *Chicken,* but he still went.

'Look, Terri, we both know Paul is a prat,' Kate declared the minute she and the sister were alone, 'and Admin live on a totally different planet to the rest of us. There's nothing I can do about Paul—he's a hopeless case—but if the papers for Mr Nicolson have gone missing I'll simply send Admin up another set, and that will keep them happy.'

'But the nurses?' Terri demanded. 'What about the nurses?'

'We'll manage,' Kate insisted. 'We've done it before, and I've no doubt we'll do it again, so come clean. What's *really* wrong? And I don't want any more twaddle about Paul or Admin.'

'It's…' The sister pulled a handkerchief out of her pocket and blew her nose noisily. 'It's Neil. He left his mobile phone at home this morning, so Frank said he'd take it round to him before he went to work.'

'And?' Kate prompted as more tears filled Terri's eyes.

'When Frank got to the pub, Neil wasn't there. Neil hasn't been there since he handed in his notice a month ago.'

'But…?'

'Exactly.' Terry nodded. 'Apparently, he only worked at the pub for two days, but he's been getting up early every morning, supposedly heading for the pub, then going God knows where.'

'Maybe he's got another job,' Kate suggested tentatively. 'Maybe he didn't like working at the pub, but as it was his dad who got him the work he didn't like to admit it because…because he was afraid Frank would be hurt.'

'Nice try, Kate,' Terri replied, 'but it's not very likely, is it? Neil's got no qualifications, he doesn't know anyone who could offer him work, and yet for the past three weeks he's been flashing money around like there's no tomorrow, so what's he *doing?*'

Kate didn't know, and she wanted to guess less. There were

so many temptations for young people nowadays, so many ways they could go off the rails, and none of them were good.

'Terri—'

'I keep thinking, what if he's shoplifting?' the sister interrupted. 'What if—dear lord, Kate—what if he's dealing drugs?'

'He wouldn't—he's not the type,' Kate said with more certainty than she felt, and Terri shook her head.

'You know as well as I do that there isn't 'a type'. It can happen to anyone. Look at Duncan Hamilton. He was a grade A student, but that didn't keep him out of the hands of the drug dealers, did it?'

It hadn't, and when Kate thought of Neil swallowing packets of cocaine as Duncan Hamilton had done, of him perhaps being rushed into her own A and E…

'Terri, I think you should talk to Mario about this,' she said quickly. 'Tell him what you've told me—'

'Are you out of your mind?' Terri interrupted, horror plain on her face. 'No way am I going to shop my own son to somebody who works in the drugs squad.'

'But, Terri—'

'Frank and I will deal with this on our own, so promise me you won't say anything to Mario—*promise.*'

More secrets, more lies, Kate thought unhappily as she stared back at the sister, but Neil wasn't her son and if Terri didn't want Mario to know about him she had to respect the sister's wishes.

'OK, I promise,' she said reluctantly, and Terri blew her nose again.

'I'm sorry—so sorry—for landing all of this on you on your birthday. I haven't forgotten,' Terri added as Kate shook her head dismissively. 'Neither have the rest of the staff. Your cards and present are in the nurses' staffroom, and I meant to take them through to your office so they'd be there when you came on duty, but then Frank phoned to tell me about Neil, and…'

'It honestly doesn't matter,' Kate said firmly, and gave the sister a hug.

It was all she could do. That, and pray Neil had somehow managed to acquire a lot of money legally.

'What's wrong with Terri?' Mario asked when Kate eventually joined him. 'She seemed really upset.'

'She's just a bit annoyed with her son, that's all,' Kate replied, and Mario frowned.

'That will be Neil. Eighteen years old, just left school?'

'How did…? Oh, of course.' Kate nodded. 'You have a file on everyone, don't you?'

'As I keep telling you, we only have detailed files on known members of the drugs fraternity,' Mario replied. 'I checked the police data base for Terri simply as a matter of routine, and it said she was married, with two kids, and gave their names and ages.'

'Oh. Right,' Kate said. 'So, who's first up in the waiting room?'

'Terri seems to be somewhat excessively upset for somebody who's simply annoyed with her son,' Mario observed, and Kate felt her cheeks heat up.

That was the trouble with getting involved with a cop. They had suspicion inbuilt in their personality, and she hated lying, was hopeless at it, but she'd promised Terri she'd say nothing, and she couldn't go back on her word.

'Terri worries a lot,' she said. 'I understand it goes with the territory if you have teenagers.'

'Uh-huh,' Mario murmured. 'So why do I have the feeling you're not telling me everything?'

'Because you're paranoid, that's why,' Kate replied, taking refuge in exasperation.

'Maybe.'

'Look, can't you stop being a cop for even two seconds?' she exclaimed, and Mario shook his head.

'Nope.'

'Then, *try*,' she said with more emphasis than she'd intended, and walked quickly over to join Paul before Mario could ask any more questions she didn't want to answer.

'We have a possibly fractured arm in the waiting room, an elderly lady complaining of earache, and somebody with stomach pains who will no doubt turn out to be suffering from nothing more serious than a bad case of indigestion,' the specialist registrar reported when he saw her. 'And to think I specialised in A and E medicine for this.'

'Hey, look on the bright side, Paul,' Kate said tartly. 'I'm sure some poor unfortunate will arrive soon with something more challenging for you, but in the meantime which patient—?'

'Did Terri tell you she forgot to send the referral forms up to IC for that mushroom case?' Paul interrupted. 'Now, far be it for me to complain…'

But you're going to, Kate thought.

'But I don't think her mind is on the job.'

Not at the moment, it isn't, Kate thought, but at least Terri would get back to her normal professional self whereas her specialist registrar was always going to be a jerk.

'How is Mr Nicolson?' she said, deliberately changing the subject.

'He's had to be put on the liver transplant list.'

'I'm sorry to hear that,' she said, and Paul shrugged.

'The man was an idiot, Kate.'

And I'm *seriously* beginning to dislike you, she thought, but she didn't say that.

'Which of the patients would you like?' she said instead, and his lip curled.

'If I were in charge, I'd bounce the lot of them out the door as timewasters.'

'But you're not in charge, are you, Paul?' she exclaimed, 'so

I suggest you take the stomach pains, and I'll take the possible fractured arm and earache.'

And in future keep your big mouth shut, she thought as the specialist registrar strode away, his face dark with ill-suppressed anger.

'A regular little Prince Charming, isn't he?' Mario observed, clearly having overheard everything Paul said.

'I can't decide whether he needs a complete personality transplant,' Kate replied, 'or a swift boot up the backside.'

'What he wants is your job,' Mario observed, 'but heaven help the staff and patients of any A and E he's ever in charge of.'

'Amen to that,' Kate observed. 'And speaking of A and E,' she continued, 'we have a possibly fractured arm waiting for us unless, of course, you're far too grand to assist me with such a mundane thing?'

'Me, grand?' Mario echoed. 'Nah. Common as muck, that's me.'

And a godsend on a day which, after a very peaceful start, turned out to be one of the busiest Kate could ever remember.

'Do you think the entire population of Aberdeen has suddenly developed a death wish?' she demanded after a lunch which had consisted of one half-eaten sandwich consumed on the run.

'Maybe they just all want to wish you happy birthday.' Mario grinned, and she shook her head at him.

'Yeah. Right. You know, I never thought I'd miss Paul,' she continued, 'but we sure as shooting could have done with his help this afternoon. Do you think he might have put a hex on us before he went off to his cousin's wedding to ensure we'd be inundated?'

'I wouldn't be at all surprised,' Mario replied. 'In fact, I'd bet money he's probably made wax images of the pair of us, and is sticking pins into them even as we speak.'

She laughed. 'Jumbo sized pins. Pins so big that…'

She came to a halt. The doors of the treatment room had slammed open and a young man was standing there, wide-eyed and sweating, his hands clenched tightly onto a wheelchair in which a young woman sat ashen-faced with pain.

'Can somebody help me, please?' he yelled. 'It's my wife, Alison. She's having a baby!'

'You need Maternity, Mr…Mr…?' Kate began, hurrying towards him only to realise that Mario and Terri were doing the same.

'My name's Mackintosh,' the young man replied. 'Ben Mackintosh, and I don't think Alison's going to make it there.'

Kate didn't think she would either when she lifted the young woman's skirt.

'Yikes, but her cervix is already fully dilated!' she exclaimed. 'Terri, phone Maternity and tell them we need someone down here fast. Mario, how much maternity experience have you had?'

'None,' he replied as Terri sped away.

'What do you mean—none?' Kate hissed.

'Exactly what I said,' he replied in the same caustic undertone. 'When I was a junior doctor I watched two births, but other than that, zilch, *nada*, none. All the pregnant women who came into hospital when I was an A and E doctor managed to make it to Maternity.'

'Well this one certainly isn't going to,' Kate muttered before fixing what she hoped was a suitably encouraging smile to her lips and turning to Ben and Alison Mackintosh. 'I'm afraid there's no time to transfer you to Maternity, so if you'd both like to come through here…'

'This is not what we planned,' Ben Mackintosh declared, wiping his forehead with a shaking hand as Mario swiftly wheeled his wife into cubicle 3, then slipped on a protective, sterile apron before helping the young mother-to-be up onto the examination trolley. 'Alison's not due for another two weeks, you see. In fact, we were at a wedding, and Alison just thought she had backache, then her waters broke when we were on our way to the reception, and—'

'Oh, cripes, but this hurts!' Alison Mackintosh exclaimed, gripping Mario's hand as though it was a lifeline. 'This really—*really*—hurts.'

'OK, Alison, we want you to push when we tell you to push, and relax when we tell you to relax, and in between times huff, puff, and pant like a dog.'

He proceeded to give the young woman a demonstration and Alison looked at him then at Kate who burst out laughing before she could stop herself.

'Mario, you sound like a constipated seal,' she protested as she reached for her protective apron, and he gave her a very hard stare.

'Look, I'm doing my best, here,' he declared, 'but never having given birth I'm at a bit of a disadvantage.'

Alison let out a laugh, that was very quickly overtaken by a groan, and swiftly Kate went to the foot of the examination trolley.

'Huff, puff, and push as Nurse Volante said, Alison,' she ordered. 'Well done—well done—now relax, and wait until you feel another contraction before you start pushing again.'

'Should it be hurting quite as much as this?' Ben Mackintosh said, whitening visibly as his wife let out a cry that was halfway between a scream and a groan.

'It won't be much longer now,' Kate declared. 'In fact—'

Her eyes fled to Mario with dismay. The baby's head hadn't crowned yet, but she could definitely feel the umbilical cord. It was presenting in front of the baby and in Maternity they would immediately have performed a Caesarean but she possessed neither the skill nor the experience to do one. She was going to have to do something, however, because if she didn't the cord would gradually become more and more compressed as the baby was born and eventually its oxygen supply would be cut off completely.

'What is it—what's wrong?' Ben Mackintosh said, glancing from Kate to Mario with concern.

'It's nothing,' Kate said reassuringly as Mario came round to the foot of the examination trolley to join her, but Ben Mackintosh wasn't convinced.

'Something's wrong—I know there is!' he exclaimed. 'What is it—what's happened?'

'Just a small hiccup,' Kate declared. 'Your baby's umbilical cord is trying to come out first.'

She heard Mario's sharp intake of breath, but to her relief Ben Mackintosh didn't.

Think, Kate, *think*, she told herself as Mario gazed impotently at her, clearly indicating that she was on her own with this one. She was sure she'd read somewhere that sometimes it was possible to push the cord up and out of the way, while holding the baby's head up. It would be as uncomfortable as hell for Alison, and she might not be able to do it, but if she did nothing…

'OK, Alison, try not to push for a few seconds,' she ordered, and the girl shook her head.

'I'm sorry, but I don't think I can,' she gasped. 'This baby…wants… *Oh, hell*, here comes another contraction…it doesn't want to wait.'

Neither did Kate, but she had to until Alison had stopped pushing and then, as gently as she could, she slipped her hand as high up as she could into the girl's vagina. The baby's head was there, and so was the cord, pulsing with life, and tentatively she tried to push the cord up and away from the baby's face.

'Relax, Alison,' Mario said soothingly. 'Just relax. Don't push.'

'I'm…sorry!' Alison exclaimed. 'But I'm going…to…have to.'

And she pushed down again, and Kate bit her lip as she felt her hand being crushed with the strength of the contraction, but she held on to the cord, and when Alison stopped pushing she was still holding it.

'The head's crowning, Kate,' Mario muttered, and she nodded.

'When it comes out try to keep the baby's head as high as you can,' she said, wincing, as Alison started to bear down again.

She wasn't going to be able to hold onto the cord for much longer. It was beginning to pull against her, and Mario must have sensed it because he leant over Alison, his face encouraging and determined.

'OK, Alison, let's go for the big one,' he declared. 'Do my constipated seal act. Relax, relax, and then I want you to push like hell.'

Alison did as he asked, and suddenly not only did the baby's head appear, but also a hand and an elbow and both shoulders.

'Great, Alison, just great!' he exclaimed, and Kate could see beads of perspiration on his forehead. 'One more push—as big as the last one—just one more…'

'Oh, *God*, never again,' the girl replied, her face scarlet. 'No more children—*ever*.'

But she bore down again and suddenly, with a slide and a rush, the baby shot out into Mario's waiting hands.

'A girl,' he declared. 'You have a beautiful baby girl, Alison.'

'Two arteries present in the cord?' Kate said quickly, flexing her fingers to try to restore some feeling into them, and Mario nodded as he clamped it.

'Just the placenta to deliver,' he said, pressing gently on Alison's uterus to help the placenta on its way and, as though on cue, a small gush of blood came from the girl, followed quickly by the placenta.

'I don't know what to say,' Ben Mackenzie said, his eyes very bright, his voice choked. 'What you just did—both of you— I… I… All I can say is thank you. *Thank you*.'

Vigorously he shook Mario's hand, then turned to Kate, and she backed up a step.

'I don't think so, do you?' she said, looking ruefully down at her fingers, and he laughed but Mario didn't.

Mario's eyes were fixed on the little girl as he wrapped her in a towel.

'Isn't she beautiful, Kate?' he said, his voice soft, husky. 'Isn't she the most beautiful baby you've ever seen?'

'Anyone would think you'd never seen a newborn before,' she protested with a chuckle, and Mario shook his head.

'Not this newborn, I haven't,' he murmured and, as he gently stroked the little girl's cheek, Kate's breath suddenly caught and wedged somewhere in the centre of her chest.

He looked so right holding Alison Mackenzie's daughter, as though he was the proud father, not Ben Mackenzie, and his face… All too often it was marred by a world-weary cynicism but there was no cynicism in his face as he handed the little girl to her mother. Instead there was a tenderness so warm, a longing so obvious, that tears sprang into Kate's eyes and she had to blink rapidly to keep them at bay.

'She really *is* special, isn't she?' Ben Mackenzie declared proudly. 'Are you a father yourself, Doctor?'

'No, I'm not,' Mario replied.

'You should try it!' Ben exclaimed, and Mario shook his head.

'I'd have to be married first, or in a long-term relationship, and I've no plans for either.'

Of course he hadn't, Kate thought as the specialist registrar from Maternity appeared with his staff, and slapped Mario on the back, clearly assuming he was the doctor in charge. He'd told her repeatedly that he didn't do long term, he didn't do commitment, so why had she felt such a shaft of pain at his words? Why had she wanted to yell, *But what about me?*

Because she'd been stupid, so stupid, she realised as Mario grinned across at her, and she managed to smile back. She'd thought herself so clever, so smart. She'd told herself she could have a casual fling with this man, then walk away with no regrets but she couldn't. He had been right, and she had been wrong, and if he left—when he left—she was going to be devastated. Devastated because somehow, some way, she'd fallen in love with him, and now she was in trouble, big trouble.

'Sorry about that, Kate,' Mario declared as the maternity staff whisked the Mackenzies away. 'I guess—because I'm a man—that guy just assumed—'

'It doesn't matter,' she interrupted with difficulty. 'It isn't important.'

And it wasn't, she thought. What *was* important was that she was going to have to end their relationship. She was going to have to tell him that it was all over, that it wasn't working, because the longer she remained involved with him the greater her heartbreak was going to be when it ended.

But not tonight, she thought, as she stared back at him. Not tonight when he'd got up so early this morning to string birthday balloons all over her sitting room walls. Not tonight after he'd bought her a present and ordered pepperoni and noodles for her birthday dinner. Tomorrow. She would end it tomorrow.

Chicken, her heart whispered, and unconsciously she shook her head. It wasn't cowardice that was making her want to wait until tomorrow, she knew it wasn't. It was something altogether worse.

'It *is* important, Kate,' Mario insisted, clearly misinterpreting the shake of her head. 'Hell, you did all the tough stuff and that guy shouldn't automatically have awarded me the credit because I'm a man. I'll go after him—explain—'

'Mario, it doesn't matter whether you did it, I did it, or a passing monkey did it,' she retorted, her aching heart making her sharper than she'd intended. 'All that matters is Alison and her daughter are OK.'

He wasn't convinced. She could see in his eyes that he wasn't convinced but, to her relief, she could also see Paul striding down the treatment room towards them. A relief that very quickly turned to surprise when she remembered he wasn't supposed to be here, and he also looked uncharacteristically panic-stricken.

'Alison Mackenzie,' he demanded. 'Is she here—is she all right?'

'She's just gone up to Maternity with her daughter and husband,' Kate replied in confusion, and saw Paul's face crumple. 'Do…do you know her?'

'She's my kid sister,' he replied. 'When she didn't turn up at the wedding reception I thought there must have been an accident, but then our mother said Ben had phoned to say Alison's waters had broken in the car and he was bringing her here. I went up to Maternity, but they said she was in A and E, and…'

'She's fine, Paul,' Kate said softly. 'She had a cord prolapse but both she and the baby are doing fine. I managed to push the cord back in until Mario could help the baby out, and—'

'So Nurse Volante rode to the rescue again, did he?' Paul interrupted. 'My, my, but you really are turning out to be a regular knight in shining armour, aren't you, Mario?'

'Now, just a minute, Paul,' Kate began angrily, but he didn't give her one.

Instead he shook her hand before she'd even realised what he was going to do, then nodded grudgingly at Mario.

'I guess I owe you both, don't I?' he said. 'Alison… Like I said, she's my kid sister, and this baby was her first, so… Well, thanks.'

And, before either of them could reply, he'd walked away, leaving Mario gazing after him in disbelief.

'Is that it?' he exclaimed. 'We deal with a life threatening situation, you have your hand damn near mangled up his sister's vagina, and that's the best he can come up with? Well, it's not good enough. I'll wring a proper thank you out of that pompous, arrogant, son of a—'

'Mario, leave it,' Kate declared, catching hold of his arm as he made to follow the specialist registrar. 'It's as much of a thank you as we're ever going to get from Paul.'

'But, Kate…'

'OK, so it was a feeble thank you,' she conceded, 'but for Paul to thank us at all is pretty damn amazing, and I guarantee one thing. He won't forget what we did. He might not like the fact that it was us who helped his sister, but in his own arrogant, pompous way he's a fair man, and he won't forget it.'

'I suppose so,' Mario said reluctantly, 'but I'd still like to squeeze a better thank you out of him.'

'And I said *leave* it,' she said, more curtly than he'd ever heard her, but when his eyebrows rose she forced a laugh. 'It's really sweet of you to want to be my knight in shining armour, but there's no need. I can take care of myself.'

No, you can't, he wanted to reply, but he didn't and it wasn't because she'd just chewed his head off twice in the space of fifteen minutes—hell, he was used to her fiery temper. It was the blankness he could see in her eyes, the bleakness, that stopped him and he was relieved when their shift finally came to an end.

He was even more relieved when he accompanied her into her office to collect her handbag, and they found a birthday cake, complete with thirty-five candles, and two cards and a small wrapped present sitting on her desk.

'I told you your staff wouldn't forget,' he observed. 'And, best of all, your cake's a plain sponge one with no marzipan or icing, so you can eat it.'

'All my staff know about my allergy so none of them would be dumb enough to give me a cake that had almonds in it,' she murmured.

'What did they get you as a present?' he asked, willing her to smile, to snap out of whatever was so clearly bothering her. 'Hey, that's neat,' he added when she unwrapped it and a pencil sharpener in the shape of a syringe emerged.

'It's from Terri,' she said. 'We always get each other joke presents for our birthdays.'

So, how come you're not laughing? he wanted to ask, but didn't.

'And the cards?' he said.

'One will be from my staff, and the other will be from Terri. Oh, that's nice of them,' she added as she opened the cards, and a voucher slipped out of one. 'My staff got me two presents this year—the cake, and an all-day session at *Tranquillity*.'

'Which is?'

'A beauty salon where they steam you, and pummel you, and wax your legs and bikini line.'

'This is a good present?' he protested, wincing, and to his relief she smiled.

'The very best if you're a girl.'

'I'll take your word for it,' he said, lifting the cake. 'And now can we go home so I can start doing all the wonderful things to you that I promised?'

And make love to you until you tell me what's wrong, he thought, as she nodded, and he drove her home.

'Are you sure you want a slice of your birthday cake right now?' he said, drawing Kate back against his chest and stretching lazily under the duvet.

'Mario, all I had at lunch time was half a sandwich and I'm starving!' she exclaimed, and he chuckled.

'Your fault for flaunting,' he murmured into her hair. 'I fully intended waiting until after dinner to make love to you, but you looked so gorgeous and luscious when we got home that food became the last thing on my mind.'

'Well, it's on my mind now,' she replied, 'and I want a slice of that birthday cake.'

'You'll get crumbs in the bed.'

'Mario…'

'OK—OK, I'm going,' he said, throwing back the duvet, and

padding towards the bedroom door. 'Stay where you are, and stay naked.'

'Your wish is my command, oh, caped—and at the moment extremely nude—crusader,' she said and he smiled when he saw her eyes dancing as she sat up and pulled the duvet round her.

Maybe he should just forget about asking her what had been wrong this afternoon, he decided as he went into the kitchen. She seemed fine now, and their love-making had been absolutely incredible. In fact, she'd held onto him so tightly that he wouldn't be at all surprised if he was covered with bruises tomorrow, but he didn't care. Just so long as she was happy again, he didn't care.

'Do you want to be really decadent and have wine with your cake?' he called as he retrieved a knife from the cutlery drawer.

'Why not?' she shouted back. 'And don't forget to light all my birthday candles.'

He shook his head and laughed. She was the Kate he knew again, so he'd say nothing. She was always telling him he possessed a cop's overly suspicious mind, and maybe on this occasion she was right.

'You'd better make your wish fast before the house burns down,' he observed as he carried the tray with the lighted birthday cake into the bedroom.

'Oh, *very* funny,' she replied. 'Hold the tray closer to me.'

He did as she asked, and she shut her eyes for a second, then blew out the candles filling the bedroom with the scent of burnt wax.

'What did you wish for?' he asked, as he put down the tray and reached for the knife.

For a second he thought he saw her eyes darken, but just as his eyebrows snapped down she smiled up at him.

'Can't tell,' she said. 'If you tell it doesn't come true.'

'Big kid.' He grinned.

'And you're not?' she exclaimed, but as she opened her mouth to take a bite of her cake he put out his hand to stop her.

'I just want to say happy birthday, Kate,' he said softly, 'and may you have many, many more of them.'

'If they all come to an end with me in bed with a Neanderthal pervert, I'll drink to that,' she said, and bit into the cake and swallowed.

Years later he would remember that moment. Years later his dreams would still be haunted by those few seconds when one minute Kate was smiling up at him, and the next the cake had fallen from her hands and she was clutching her throat.

'What is it—what's wrong?' he cried, but he knew.

It might have been years since he'd treated a case of anaphylactic shock, but he recognised the symptoms immediately and, without even waiting for her reply, he sprinted out of the bedroom and into the bathroom, sending her face creams and shampoo clattering into the sink as he grabbed her syringe from the bathroom cabinet.

By the time he got back to the bedroom her lips were double their normal size, and she was making the most awful gasping, gulping sounds that he had ever heard a human being make.

'Thigh,' she gasped through a throat that was already closing. 'Thigh…'

He yanked the duvet off her and, with a hand that had suddenly become frighteningly all fingers and thumbs, he pulled the black needle cap from the syringe, snapped the safety cap from the firing button, then held the Anapen against her outer thigh, and prayed as he had never prayed before.

Slowly—far too slowly for him—her breathing began to ease, and when she finally managed a small wobbly smile he caught her to him and held her tight, all too aware that he was shaking, but completely unable to stop himself.

'*Madre di Dio, Kate*, I thought…I thought…'

'I'm all right—I'm all right!' she exclaimed breathlessly, but he could feel her heart thundering against his chest, and he shook his head.

'You need to go to hospital. I'll help you dress—'

'No—no hospital,' she replied with difficulty. 'All they'll do is collect urine from me every couple of hours and test it for methyl histamine. I can do that for myself at home.'

'But, Kate—'

'Mario, you know what people are like,' she continued, talking over him. 'They say they understand. They say that having an allergy isn't a problem, but if I go into hospital—even for a night—Admin will note it down on my file, and I don't want there to be any suggestion or implication that I'm not fit for my job.'

'*Dio*, Kate, I don't give a damn about your job!' he exclaimed, his voice hoarse, constricted. 'Do you have any idea of how much you scared me? I thought I'd lost you. I thought…'

'Mario, I'm all right,' she insisted, but he didn't believe her, she could see he didn't, and she caught hold of his hands and held them tight. 'You thought I was going to die like Antonia, didn't you?'

'I thought…' He bit his lip savagely. 'I thought I'd failed you, just as I failed her.'

'Failed me?' she repeated in confusion. 'Mario what…what actually happened to Antonia?'

For a second she didn't think he was going to answer, then he took a ragged breath.

'She died of an overdose.'

'You mean, she was on medication for something?' she faltered. 'That she made a mistake?'

'No, I don't mean that,' he said bleakly. 'Antonia and I… We met in the A and E department of the Royal Infirmary in Edinburgh on our first day at work as newly qualified doctors, and we just sort of clicked. She… She was so special, Kate. So full of life, so full of fun and joy.'

And you still love her, Kate thought, feeling her heart ache at the tenderness she could see in his face.

'Go on,' she forced herself to say.

'We became lovers, and I was so happy, so very happy. Both our careers were going well, and though she had to transfer to another hospital to become a specialist registrar, it didn't matter. We were living together so we saw each other every day, and then…' He bit his lip savagely. 'I discovered she was taking amphetamines. She said her job was so stressful that she needed them.'

'That's why you said Colin should quit now,' she declared with dawning comprehension. 'You think he's going to find A and E too hard, that he might start taking uppers to cope?'

He nodded, his face dark.

'She promised she wouldn't take them any more, Kate, and I'd joined the police force by then, was working all the hours God sends trying to prove I was up to it, so I thought she was telling me the truth, but one day…' He swallowed convulsively. 'I'd finished my shift earlier than I'd expected, so I went home, carrying a big bottle of wine and some flowers to make up for all the times I'd been late, and I found her injecting cocaine in the bathroom.'

'Oh, Mario!' she exclaimed. 'What did you do?'

'Went through the roof,' he said grimly. 'Told her she was killing herself, and that if she didn't care about that she should think about me, her family, her friends. I thought I'd got through to her, but when I came home the next day she'd gone. Taken all of her clothes and just gone. I went round to the hospital to talk to her, and discovered she'd been suspended the week before. Somebody had seen her injecting in one of the staff toilets, and she was due at a meeting for unprofessional conduct that day but she never showed up.'

'What…what happened then?' she asked softly, and he closed his eyes, his face all dark planes and shadows.

'I called all her friends, her family—everybody I knew—but nobody could tell me where she was. I scoured the streets for weeks, looking for her, but it was one of the beat police who eventually found her, dead in a seedy hostel. She'd choked on her own vomit, and when they did the autopsy they…they discovered she'd been pregnant, pregnant with my son.'

'Mario, I'm so sorry,' she whispered. 'So very, very sorry.'

'I failed her, Kate,' he said, his voice bleak. 'When she needed me most, I failed her.'

'But you didn't fail her,' she protested. 'Sometimes… Sometimes people don't want to be helped. Sometimes you can give and give, but if they don't want that help, don't take the hand you're holding out to them, there's nothing you can do.'

'Maybe,' he muttered, but when he got to his feet and reached for his clothes she eased herself up onto her pillows as quickly as her aching body would allow.

'Where are you going?' she exclaimed. 'I told you I'm not going into hospital—'

'I need to phone Ralph, get him round here.'

'But why?' she protested, and Mario swore under his breath as he pulled on his denims.

'Kate, don't you realise even yet what has just happened? The person who left that cake in your office *knew* what would happen if you ate it, but only your closest friends and staff know you're allergic to almonds, so…'

'Somebody I know has told the drug dealers about my allergy,' she finished for him faintly.

'Exactly.'

'George,' she murmured without thinking, and saw Mario's eyebrows snap down. 'The new porter. He's always staring at me. I know I should have told you this before, but I thought I was just overreacting, being stupid. His full name's George Luciano but Terri and I call him the incredible hulk.'

'I must remember to tell him that. He's one of my men, Kate,' Mario continued with a faint smile as she stared at him in confusion. 'I knew I couldn't stay close to you all the time at work so I arranged for Bill to get the windfall he needed to go to New Zealand courtesy of police funds and then put George in his place to keep an eye on you.'

'Oh. Right.' She smiled awkwardly. 'Sorry.'

'Don't be,' he said, 'and keep those ideas coming.' He buttoned his shirt, then paused. 'Kate, I…' He shook his head impatiently. 'There's no easy way to say this so I might just as well come right out and say it. I can't stay with you any more.'

'But I thought you said you had to, to keep me safe,' she said before she could stop herself, and his face convulsed.

'I *can't* stay, Kate. Don't you see that? If I stay I'll get too involved with you—*Madre di Dio*, I already am—and if the thought of losing you terrifies me now, how much worse is it going to be if I allow myself to fall in love with you?'

'Falling in love is always scary, Mario,' she said, her eyes fixed on him, 'but that doesn't mean we should all become hermits.'

'That's easy for you to say,' he flared. 'You've never lost someone you loved more than life itself.'

'No, but—'

'I'll let you down, Kate. I'll fail you like I've failed every other woman in my life. I wouldn't want to—wouldn't intend to—but it would happen, and I can't do that to you—I won't.'

'But, Mario—'

'I'll get George to move in here with you,' he interrupted. 'And, yes, I do know he looks intimidating,' he added as she opened her mouth, clearly intending to protest, 'but that's exactly the kind of person I want watching out for you.'

'Right,' she said.

'Kate…' He thrust his fingers through his hair, his face taut. 'I'm sorry.'

'It's all right,' she said with a brave attempt at a smile. 'You said no promises, no commitment, and I agreed, didn't I, and maybe…maybe it's better this way.'

His eyes met hers, bleak and dark and desolate. 'I truly am sorry, Kate.'

And as he walked out of her bedroom, and gently closed the door, she bit down hard on her lip to stop herself from calling him back and begging him to reconsider because he was right.

It was better if it ended this way. She was a workaholic, and he was in love with a ghost, and a relationship like that could only ever end in disaster. So it was better if they finished it now, but it didn't feel better as she sat alone in her empty bedroom feeling her heart break. Perhaps it would, eventually. One day. But it didn't feel better right now.

CHAPTER EIGHT

HE SHOULD never have made love to her, Mario decided as he watched Kate walk across the treatment room to talk to Terri. He should never have allowed himself to be talked into it, and once he had he sure as shooting shouldn't have continued doing it. It had been a mistake—a big one—but thank heavens he'd come to his senses before he'd broken Kate's heart.

And he obviously hadn't broken it. Not by a word, or even the slightest look, had she hinted since he'd moved out of her flat five days ago that she considered him a low life scumbag. Which was great. Really great, because only a rat with a super-sized ego would have wanted her to miss him.

But he was a rat, he realised, as he felt a wave of something he couldn't quite identify clog his throat when he saw her face light up at whatever Terri had said, because he thought she might have missed him. Just a little bit.

Dio, but he missed her, and it wasn't just the sex, wonderful though that had been. He missed so many stupid, unimportant things. Like their arguments over whether they should have a home-cooked dinner or a takeaway after work. Like seeing her small feet resting beside his size elevens on the coffee table when they watched TV. Like never being able to find his razor amongst all her creams and lotions, or laughing at something she'd said or done, and it was crazy. *Crazy*.

'Miss Thornton—the elderly lady with localised epigastric pain, no bowel sounds and high fever?' Kate declared as she walked towards him. 'She definitely has a perforated peptic ulcer. She's just back from X-ray, and the plates have confirmed it.'

'Do you want me to page OR, let them know she's on her way?' he asked, and Kate nodded.

'Please,' she said, then her eyes sparkled. 'The big question, of course, is who's going to tell her? Terri and I were just debating whether I should do it as I was the one who examined her, or whether I should let Paul have the pleasure.'

'Well…' Mario frowned as though giving her question serious consideration. 'On balance, having weighed up the pros and cons, I'd say, land Paul with the hot potato.'

'She *is* a bit of a battleaxe, isn't she?' Kate chuckled.

'I can't decide whether my favourite moment was when she asked you whether you were fully qualified,' Mario observed, 'or if it's when she said she wished you'd stop asking such damn fool questions, and let the experts in X-ray decide what was wrong with her.'

'Yup, it's a close call between the two.' Kate laughed. 'But I don't think even Paul deserves Miss Thornton so do you want to join me when I break the news to her, or would you rather head for the hills?'

I'd rather hold you, he thought, and though he tried to stamp on the thought it wouldn't go away. Just as no amount of reminding himself over the past five days that he would only hurt her, make her unhappy, had stopped him thinking about her. Constantly.

'Mario?'

Kate was staring at him hesitantly, and he dredged up a smile.

'Let's beard the lioness in her den,' he said.

'So, I'm definitely going to need an operation?' Miss Thornton declared when Kate broke the news.

'Operations for perforated peptic ulcers aren't nearly as

serious as they used to be,' Kate replied, watching the elderly lady closely. 'And you look to be in good physical shape.'

'For my age, you mean,' Miss Thornton said dryly. 'Well, let's get on with it.'

'Did anybody come in with you? I'm not being nosy,' Kate added as the elderly lady frowned, 'but if you have a friend or a relative waiting outside we'd better let them know what's happening.'

'Not married, no immediate family,' Miss Thornton declared. 'Phoned for a taxi myself when my stomach started to hurt.'

Kate turned to beckon to George, then paused. She was sure she'd seen a flicker of fear in the old lady's eyes when she'd told her she would have to have an operation. It had only been there for a second, but she was certain it had been there, and quickly she turned back to the trolley.

'You'll be fine—I promise,' she said softly, reaching out to clasp Miss Thornton's hand in hers. 'And after your operation, when they take you up to Women's Surgical, I want you to give them hell for me, OK?'

A small smile curved the elderly lady's lips.

'You think they need it?'

'I *know* they do,' Kate whispered, and the smile on Miss Thornton's lips widened.

'Then it will be my mission to do the best I can, and if you should ever find yourself near Women's Surgical while I'm there, and have nothing better to do…'

'You think I'm not going to visit you?' Kate protested. 'Wild horses wouldn't keep me away.'

'See that they don't,' Miss Thornton declared, then frowned irritably. 'Well, am I going to have this operation or not?'

And Kate chuckled as the old lady was wheeled out of A and E, but as she turned to walk over to the whiteboard she suddenly realised Mario was watching her.

'That was a kind thing to do,' he said, and Kate shrugged.

'I'll be old one day myself, and no doubt in exactly Miss Thornton's position with no family to bolster my courage, so it's no big deal for me to visit her. Plus I liked her.'

'I liked her, too.'

I like you, he thought. It was odd but he'd never once asked himself whether he liked Antonia. He'd known he'd loved her, but he'd never once asked himself whether he'd actually liked her, and why he should suddenly find himself wondering about that was beyond him.

'I…I'd better clean out the cubicle,' he said, backing up a step as Terri joined them.

'Don't rush away on my account,' the sister replied, but he'd already gone and Terri squared her jaw.

'Look, I know this is absolutely none of my business,' she declared, 'but what's going on?'

'I was going to ask you the same thing,' Kate said lightly. 'Has Neil revealed yet how he's earning all his money?'

'All he'll tell us is that he's earning it legally and don't try to change the subject.'

'I'm not trying to change any subject,' Kate protested, and Terri let out a huff of impatience.

'Yeah, right. So are you going to tell me why you and Mario used to be the best of friends, and now there's this really weird atmosphere between you?'

'You mean, we're shouting at one another?'

'No, but—'

'Ignoring one another, being sarcastic, cutting one another dead?'

'You're not doing any of those things,' Terri conceded, 'but something's different, something's changed. I thought at one time that maybe the two of you might—you know—but now…'

'Oh, good heavens, no,' Kate said with a bright laugh. 'He's only here because of his work, and though we get on well together we could never be anything but friends.'

And Mario had heard her, she realised, as he came out of the cubicle and strode past them without a word, but it was good that he had. Good that he knew she wasn't hurt or upset because she would rather have walked through fire than have admitted to him that every time she saw him she felt as though her heart was breaking.

'Well, I think you're both mad!' Terri exclaimed. 'You share the same sense of humour, he used to be a doctor so his eyes won't glaze over if you start talking about your work, and he's drop dead gorgeous. Hell, girl, what more do you want?'

Nothing more, Kate thought miserably as Terri walked away, but it had never been going to work, and she should have realised that.

She should have realised that even if he had eventually grown to love her he would also eventually have come to resent her job just as John had done. The bitter, corrosive arguments that had killed her ex-husband's love would have killed Mario's love, too, and she couldn't have borne it if she and Mario had grown to dislike one another as much as she and John had done. So it was better that they parted now. Better that she accepted it was never meant to be, and, if she was having difficulty in believing that at the moment, she knew one day that she would.

'Something wrong, Kate?' Paul asked, and she shook her head, forcing a bright smile to her lips.

'Everything's fine, Paul.'

He nodded, turned to walk away, then paused.

'Things can change, Kate,' he murmured awkwardly. 'People can, too. Remember that.'

And, before she could reply, the specialist registrar strode away leaving Kate staring, open mouthed, after him. Ever since she'd helped his sister she'd sensed a growing—albeit grudging—respect for her from Paul, but this... This was almost the verbal equivalent of a cuddle from Paul. OK, so she could never see them becoming best buddies, just as she couldn't ever see herself and George becoming the best of friends even though he was living with her now on Mario's orders, but she sensed life in A and E was perhaps going to be a lot easier from now on.

'Dr Kennedy, do you think I could have a word?'

Or, then again, perhaps not, Kate thought as she turned to see Colin Watson standing behind her, looking nervous, and awkward, which meant something was wrong and at the moment the last thing she needed was another problem.

'I'm really busy, Colin,' she said evasively. 'Can't it wait?'

'It won't take long. Ten—fifteen—minutes tops,' the junior doctor pressed, and she sighed inwardly.

He looked uncomfortable as well as nervous which meant she definitely wasn't going to like what he had to say but she was the consultant, he was her junior doctor, and it was her job to listen to his problems.

'Come with me,' she said, leading the way out of the treatment room and down the corridor into her office. 'And don't look so worried,' she added encouragingly when she sat down. 'I'm not an ogre, and I promise I won't bite.'

'It's about my position in A and E,' he said in a rush, clearly going for the direct let's-get-this-over-with approach. 'I've decided A and E isn't for me, and I'd like to be transferred to Men's Medical for the rest of my basic training.'

'This is a bit sudden, isn't it?' she said, completely taken aback, because whatever else she had been expecting it hadn't been that. 'I mean, have you thought this through properly, given it—?'

'Dr Kennedy, I thought A and E was what I wanted,' he interrupted, 'and it's certainly exciting but the truth is I can't do it. I thought I could, but the pressure… It's too relentless, too intense. Mario said—'

'You've spoken to him about this?' Kate broke in.

'He realised I was struggling,' Colin said, 'so we've been talking and he's suggested I might be better suited to GP work. He said that though general practice wasn't ever regarded as being glamorous, or as vital as A and E, it was actually incredibly important.'

'He's right, Colin.'

'I know.' The junior doctor nodded. 'Just as I also know that my leaving is going to make things a bit difficult for you until you can appoint my replacement.'

And how, she thought, but she would never have attempted to make him change his mind. Mario had been right. If Colin couldn't cope now he most certainly wouldn't be able to cope when she asked him to treat their more complicated cases.

'I'll be sorry to see you go,' she said, getting to her feet, 'but I respect your decision and I admire your courage for making it.'

'Mario said you'd see it that way,' the junior doctor declared, relief plain on his face.

'He did?'

Colin nodded as he followed her out of her office. 'He also said you were the best consultant he's ever worked with.'

'That…that was nice of him,' Kate said through a throat so tight it hurt. 'He…he's actually pretty terrific himself.'

Mario was, she thought, as she walked back into the treatment room and she felt her heart ache with longing as her eyes met his, but she wished with all her heart that he could solve Duncan Hamilton's case and leave because seeing him every day…

It was so hard to keep on smiling, to keep on pretending she felt nothing, but she was going to do it if it killed her. Never— *never*—was he ever going to know that she loved him. It would be too embarrassing for both of them.

'Stewart Bolton's just arrived,' Mario declared as he walked towards her. 'The bounce-back you said you wanted to see if he ever presented again?' he added helpfully. 'This time he's got chest pains, wheeziness, palpitations and hyperventilation in addition to sickness and diarrhoea. Sounds to me like he's working his way through a medical dictionary.'

It looked that way to Kate, too, after she had finished examining Mr Bolton and could find absolutely nothing wrong with him.

'And you've had these symptoms how long?' she asked, pulling her stethoscope out of her ears.

'To be honest, Doctor, I haven't felt well for the past year,' Stewart Bolton replied plaintively. 'If it hasn't been one thing, it's been another.'

And I think you're just a timewaster, she thought, and Mario was clearly thinking the same because he rolled his eyes slightly, but she couldn't risk dismissing Mr Bolton's symptoms out of hand. She had to be sure.

'I just want a quick word with my colleague, Mr Bolton,' she declared, motioning to Mario. 'I won't keep you a minute.'

'Munchausen's syndrome?' Mario asked in an undertone as soon as they were outside the cubicle. 'He just enjoys coming into hospital, the attention he gets here, so he's fabricating all these symptoms?'

'That's my diagnosis,' she replied, 'but I want to cover all bases so we'll give him a U and E, BMG, blood glucose test, and urine culture in case he's suffering from accidental poisoning, and let's toss in a CXR, CT scan and an ECG reading for good measure. That little lot should cheer him up immensely.'

But, to her surprise, when she went back into the cubicle and told Mr Bolton what she planned to do, he didn't look at all happy. In fact, he looked downright alarmed.

'Do I really need to have all those tests?' he protested. 'I thought maybe you'd just give me some pills, a pick-me-up bottle?'

'There's no need to panic, Mr Bolton,' Kate said, glancing across at Mario with a puzzled frown because a true Munchausen's syndrome patient would have been over the moon at the news. 'I only want to run the tests as a precaution. For all I know you might simply be suffering from an allergy of some kind.'

'You have an allergy, yourself, don't you, Doctor?' he observed. 'I heard some of the nurses talking about it the last time I was here,' he added as Kate gazed at him with surprise and she smiled.

'And I'm still here to tell the tale, so please stop worrying.'

'Yes, but it does mean you always have to be extra careful, doesn't it, Doctor?' Stewart Bolton continued. 'Like you obviously couldn't risk eating any of your birthday cake.'

'Actually, I did eat a bit,' Kate began. 'I was very luck—' She came to a halt. 'How did you know I had a birthday cake?'

'One of your nurses told me,' he replied with a smile that didn't quite reach his eyes, and Kate shook her head.

'They couldn't have done,' she said, her heart suddenly beginning to beat very fast. 'None of them asked me whether I enjoyed the cake, so none of them knew I had one.'

'It must have been one of the porters,' Stewart Bolton blustered, his plump cheeks becoming distinctly florid. 'Look, does it matter?'

'Yes, it matters,' Kate said slowly, 'because only three people could know I had a birthday cake. Myself, Nurse Volante and the person who got me it. You... You were the one who left that cake for me, knowing I have an allergy to almonds, knowing exactly what would happen if I ate it. It was *you*.'

'I don't know what you're talking about!' Stewart Bolton exclaimed. 'This is rid—'

'And your name's Bolton,' Kate said, with dawning, horror-stricken comprehension. '*Bolton*. I knew it was a town, but I couldn't remember which one. *Yours* is the name I couldn't remember. *Yours* is the other name that Duncan Hamilton gave me.'

Stewart Bolton sat up fast and before Kate could move Mario was standing in front of her, shielding her.

'Kate, get George.'

'But—'

'*Now*, Kate.'

And she fled, leaving Stewart Bolton staring at Mario with exasperation.

'The woman is clearly deranged!' he exclaimed. 'I'm an ordinary member of the public who came in here for medical help and—'

'Stewart Bolton,' Mario interrupted. 'I must caution you that you do not have to say anything, but anything you do say—'

'You're a cop?' Bolton interrupted in disbelief before Mario could finish. 'Then you must know—what she said—accused me of—is complete nonsense.'

'You'll have plenty of time to think about that when you're behind bars,' Mario replied, and for a moment Stewart Bolton said nothing then he smiled, a tight, confident smile.

'Only if you can prove it, and I very much doubt you'll be able to.'

'Oh, I'll prove it,' Mario declared as George swept into the cubicle closely followed by Kate. 'I'll nail you for this if it's the last thing I do.'

'You can try, Volante.' Stewart Bolton sneered. 'You can certainly try.'

And with George at his side he walked out of the treatment room, leaving Kate gazing after them, white-faced and shaking.

'It was him,' she whispered. 'All those visits to the unit… He must have been trying to find out information about me. It was him, Mario, and I just didn't realise it.'

'Kate—'

'And he was right,' she said, her voice trembling. 'You're never going to be able to prove it. A cake can't have fingerprints on it, can it, and you held the plate, and so did I, and he probably wore gloves, and—'

'Kate, I'll prove it,' Mario interrupted, hating the fear he could see in her eyes, wanting to hold her, but knowing he mustn't because if he held her… 'If it takes me to the end of my police career, I'll prove it.'

'Right.' She nodded. 'That's good. I mean, that's comforting.' She took a steadying breath. 'You must be pleased—finally getting your man. It will mean you won't have to work here any more.'

'I…I guess not.'

His face was taut, strained, and she hitched her best smile to her lips.

'Well, goodbye then. It's been…' She couldn't have said it had been nice knowing him if her very life had depended on it. 'Thanks for all your help.'

'Ralph will keep you informed about what's happening, but—'

'But you won't need to talk to me again,' she finished for him. 'I understand.'

He backed up a step, then cleared his throat. 'Kate—'

'You'd better get going,' she broke in quickly. 'George will be waiting for you.'

'Yes. I…' A muscle clenched tight at the side of his cheek. 'Well, goodbye then.'

And she nodded, and as he walked out of the unit Terri rushed up to her, her eyes agog.

'I've just seen George with that bounce-back patient,' the sister exclaimed, 'and George had the poor man in an arm lock. What happened? Did Bolton turn nasty, or something?'

'In a way,' Kate replied.

'What way?' Terri demanded, and Kate managed a small smile.

'If you've got five minutes, Terri, I'll tell you.'

'You'd better order us more steri-strips, and double our normal order of amoxicillin and clarithromycin now winter's on the horizon,' Kate declared as she and Terri stood together in the unit store cupboard. 'And it probably wouldn't do any harm to double our order of halothane. The mists in October can often trigger acute attacks in asthma patients.'

Terri nodded but, as she followed Kate out of the store cupboard and saw her rub her temples wearily, her plump face became determined.

'You're pushing yourself too hard, you know that, don't you?' she chided. 'This last month—ever since Mario left…' She shook her head. 'I know you're a workaholic, but quite frankly I'm surprised you're still standing. You practically live in the unit, you scarcely sleep—'

'I'm fine, Terri,' Kate interrupted. 'It's just been a very busy month, that's all.'

'Right.' The sister bit her lip, then glanced uncertainly at her. 'Kate, I know this is none of my business, but can't you fix whatever went wrong between you and Mario? Anyone with half a brain could see the guy was in love with you, and you'd fallen for him big time—I know you had—so why did you break up?'

'Terri, it's all water under the bridge now,' Kate replied, 'so can't you please just forget it?'

'No, I can't,' the sister said bluntly. 'I want to know what went wrong, and I won't quit bitching until you tell me.'

Terri's face had set into the stubborn lines Kate knew only too well, and she sighed. The sister wouldn't give up until she told her so maybe it was better to just get it over with, to tell her the truth, and so, slowly and haltingly, she did.

'So, you see, Terri,' she said when she'd finished. 'He's still in love with Antonia.'

'No, he's not,' the sister retorted. 'He's just terrified he will hurt you, but shutting out all human love isn't the answer, and he has to face up to that, and as for you… Mario isn't John, so why you and Mario can't simply work out these non-problems is beyond me.'

'Terri, he hasn't tried to contact me once in the last month. I think that tells you how he feels about our "non-problems", don't you?' Kate exclaimed, and to her surprise the sister smiled.

'So, if he were to suddenly turn up unexpectedly, you wouldn't want to talk to him?'

No, she wouldn't, Kate thought. She was getting through whole days now without remembering his smile, his touch, and his kiss, so she was moving on, starting to live again. OK, so she still hadn't got round to making an appointment at the hairdresser, and her fridge had been receiving rather a serious workout over the past month, but she'd put her flat on the market so she was moving on.

In a way.

'What would be the point, Terri?' she declared, suddenly re-alising that the sister was expecting an answer.

'Well, you better think of one fast,' Terri exclaimed, 'because he's just walked into the unit.'

Kate's heart lurched as it hadn't done for weeks, and she turned slowly, willing herself to feel nothing, but it was a vain hope. The minute her eyes met Mario's it was as though the last month had never happened, but never would she let him know that. She had her pride left if nothing else.

'Long time no see,' she declared, all bright and upbeat, and he shrugged awkwardly.

'I have news about the Bolton case, so I thought I'd drop by, bring you up to date.'

'Right.' She nodded. 'You're looking very smart,' she added as her gaze took in his dark navy suit, pale blue shirt and discreet tie.

Thinner, too, she thought, and tired, and had he always had those faint lines etched between his eyebrows?

His lips twitched slightly. 'What you mean is, I don't look quite so much like a bum today.'

'I never thought you looked like a bum,' she protested, and the smile on his lips widened.

'No?'

'Well, maybe I did,' she conceded, 'just a little bit.'

Out of the corner of her eye she noticed that Terri had moved away from them, clearly wanting to give them some privacy, but she wished the sister would come back. She didn't want to talk to Mario, didn't want to be reminded of what they had shared, and she most definitely didn't want to face the fact that the feelings she'd thought she'd conquered were still there, and as strong as ever.

'The Bolton case?' she continued quickly.

'I've been trying to track down the baker who made your birthday cake, and finally I found him,' Mario replied. 'Actually, it was Bolton's insistence on the cake containing almonds that proved his downfall. The baker remembered him quite clearly because it was so unusual for anyone to want almonds included in a plain sponge mixture.'

'Has Bolton admitted it was him?' she asked.

'There wasn't much else he could do when he was confronted with a positive ID. In fact, he sang like a canary, admitted he was Duncan Hamilton's fixer, and gave us names, dates and places that will enable Interpol to arrest some very big players in the drug world.'

'Your bosses must be pleased,' she observed, and Mario smiled.

'I've actually been given a commendation, but more importantly it means you won't need to testify because your evidence isn't anywhere near as damning as Bolton's.'

'That's good.' She nodded 'Well, it was kind of you to drop by and give me the news,' she continued, 'but, as you can see, I'm pretty busy—'

'How's Colin?'

'He's taken your advice, decided to become a GP.'

'He'll be good at it. And Paul?' he continued. 'How's Paul?'

'Better,' she replied. 'A lot better. He and I are never going to take part in group hugs, or anything, because that's not him, but since the birth of his niece, well, he's definitely getting better.'

'Good.'

Oh, lord, but this was awful—toe-curling—Kate thought. She and Mario had lived together, for God's sake, even if it had only been for a week. They'd been as close as two people ever could be, and now they were talking to one another like two colleagues who hadn't seen one another for ages. Two awkward, uncomfortable colleagues who had never had anything in common.

'I'd better get back to work,' she said, holding out her hand, but he didn't take it.

'Have Terri and Frank got over the fact that Neil's a male stripper?' he said instead, and Kate couldn't prevent a smile from curving her lips.

'I think Frank's still having problems with it, but Terri's OK, particularly as Neil said he only went into it because the money was so good and once he's saved up enough he's going to college to train to become an electrician.'

'That's a bit of a quantum leap, isn't it?' Mario observed, and Kate's smile widened.

'Apparently he and his fellow strippers often encounter problems with the lighting when they're doing their acts, and he's discovered he's got a real talent for fixing electrical faults.'

'Good. Great.'

'Well, like I said,' she began. 'It was kind of you to stop by—'

'I hear you've put your flat up for sale?' he interrupted, and she gazed at him in surprise.

'How did…? Oh, of course,' she said with a small smile. 'The long arm of the law.'

'No, not really,' he murmured. 'I've just been keeping an eye on you. For your own safety, of course,' he added quickly. 'In case I was wrong about the drug dealers not being interested in you any more. Why have you decided to move?'

Because my flat is full of memories of you. Because every room I go into is full of memories of you, and I can't bear it.

'I just decided that as I've never really been happy there it's crazy for me to stay,' she replied. 'And now I really *do* have to go, so if you'll excuse me…'

And before he could say anything else, she'd walked away from him, and Terri hurried after her.

'Are you *crazy?*' the sister hissed in exasperation. 'What on earth were you doing, rabbiting on about people in the department? Why didn't you say, "I miss you, Mario, I want you back"?'

'Because I don't,' Kate replied firmly.

'But, Kate—' Terri bit off what she had been about to say as they both heard the sound of running feet, then turned and smiled. 'Did you forget something, Mario?

'Actually, I was wondering whether Kate might have time for a coffee?' he replied. 'There's a café just down the road that serves pretty good cappuccino.'

He looked awkward, and flustered, and as uncomfortable as hell, but Kate steeled her resolve.

'I'm sorry, but I'm afraid—'

'Of course she has time,' Terri interrupted.

Kate shot the sister a look that spoke volumes.

'No, I don't,' she said. 'In fact—'

'Yes, you do have time,' Paul declared suddenly appearing beside them. 'I can handle anything that comes in, Kate, and if I can't I'll page you.'

Dammit, but now they'd both ganged up on her, Kate thought with irritation, but short of being downright rude there was nothing she could do.

'It will have to be a very quick coffee, then,' she declared firmly, but, as she turned to accompany Mario, Terri caught hold of her by the arm.

'Just *listen* to him, OK?' the sister whispered. 'Give him a chance, Kate, and *listen* to him.'

But I don't want to, Kate thought as she walked with Mario

out of the unit. I don't want to listen to him, I don't want to be in his company. I thought I was over him, that I was moving forward, but I'm not because it still hurts. It hurts so much.

'Actually, I don't really want a coffee, if that's OK with you?' she said as she and Mario stood outside the hospital. 'There's a park at the end of the road. Maybe we could just walk there for a bit instead?'

He nodded, but by the time they'd reached the park Kate wished she'd thought to grab her coat. The hot days they'd had in August had been succeeded by a beautiful autumn, but now the trees were bare, the leaves were lying in sodden clumps underneath them, and a chill October wind was blowing that suggested winter was not far away.

'You're cold,' Mario said, seeing her clutch her suit jacket tighter to her.

'Maybe this wasn't such a good idea,' she replied. 'In fact…maybe none of this is a very good idea.'

'Kate…'

'Mario, what do you want from me?' she demanded, and he shook his head.

'Not here. Look, there's a gazebo over there,' he continued, pointing ahead of them. 'Let's go inside and we can talk.'

She didn't want to go into the gazebo and she definitely didn't want to talk. She wanted to be back in the A and E unit, working, and trying to forget him all over again.

'OK,' she said, 'but I—'

'Can't stay long,' he finished for her. 'I know. You said.'

The gazebo was old and rusty, with a distinct odour of damp coats, and even damper leaves, but at least it was warmer than outside, and she sat down and stared out at the little pond outside where some ducks were swimming round and round in circles.

Know how you feel, she thought.

'I've missed you, Kate.'

She looked up to find Mario's eyes on her, as deep and as blue as the eyes that had been plaguing her dreams, and forced herself to smile.

'We had some good times, didn't we?' she said lightly. 'In fact, I still laugh when I remember all those male patients who thought you were gay.'

He sat down beside her, stretching his long legs out in front of him, and stared at the pond, too.

'That isn't what I remember, Kate,' he murmured. 'What I remember is you.'

'Mario—'

'No, let me finish,' he insisted. 'For the past eight years I've never allowed myself to get close to anyone because…because I was afraid that if I did I would fail them, like I failed Antonia and Sue, but this month apart…' He glanced across at her, his face tight. 'I've come to realise that I'm more afraid of never seeing you again, of never being with you again.'

'We can still see one another once in a while, if that's what you want,' she said. *Though God knows how I'll remain sane if we do.* 'We can still be friends.'

'The trouble is, I don't simply want to be friends with you, Kate,' he said, and she stirred uneasily in her seat.

'Mario, if you're trying to suggest that we should live together again… I'm sorry, but I can't. You're still in love with Antonia—'

'I'm not,' he interrupted, his eyes strained, 'I know that now. In fact, I think, if she had lived, our love would eventually have burned itself out because it was always too intense, too frantic, but when she died… I felt so guilty, and because I did I created an Antonia without faults, an Antonia who didn't ever exist except in my own imagination.'

'You weren't to blame, Mario.'

'I know that, too, now. We all have to make our own choices

in life, and I realise now that there was nothing I could have said or done that would have altered the choice she made.'

'No,' she murmured.

'Kate…' Tentatively he took one of her hands in his. 'I know I'm domineering and driven. I know I won't be the easiest man in the world to live with, but…' He swore under his breath. 'Kate, what I'm trying to say—very badly—is I know I've been a complete idiot where you're concerned, and…will you give me another chance?'

She stared up into the face she knew so well, the face she knew she would always love, but would loving him be enough? She wanted to believe it would be, but her doubts spoke louder.

'Mario, if you're driven then I'm ten times worse, and if we lived together again you'd eventually start complaining about the hours I work—'

'I wouldn't,' he interrupted. 'I couldn't, not with my own track record.'

'Which is exactly why it can't ever work,' she declared. 'After a while we'd become like ships passing in the night, and it would be me and John all over again.'

'No, it wouldn't. Listen to me, Kate,' he said, tightening his grip on her hand. 'We're not the only dedicated people in the world. There are other people just the same, and when they find someone they want to be with, they manage to make it work.'

'How?' she demanded.

'By compromising!' he exclaimed. 'It works for other people who have jobs like ours so why can't it work for us? If we both accept that our places of work won't sink without trace if we're not there twenty-four hours a day, seven days a week, then it *will* work.'

'And you honestly think we'd be able to do that?' she said with a half smile.

'I want to try.'

'Yes, but…'

He released her hands and trapped her face between his palms. '*Ti amore, Kate. Sei tutto il mio amore.*'

'That…that sounded pretty intense,' she said shakily, and a smile tugged at his lips.

'It means I love you, Kate Elizabeth Kennedy. You are my life, my heart, my soul. I think you have been ever since you waved that syringe at me and told me if I didn't back off I'd be HIV positive, too.'

Her heart turned over, and she reached up to touch his face.

'You know, I really *must* learn Italian,' she said, and he shook his head.

'And that is not an answer.'

'I…' She took a deep breath. 'I love you, too, but—' She held up her hands quickly to hold him back as he reached for her. 'Mario, I don't know if just loving you will be enough. I don't want to hurt you, to make you unhappy.'

'Kate, I'm not John. I don't want you to change. I want you to stay exactly the way you are. Infuriating, and adorable, bloody-minded, and, oh, so loveable, and as for the future…' A smile curved his lips. 'This is new for me, too, and I think all we can do is help each other through the rough times, hold one another when things get tough—'

'And never let the sun go down on our anger,' she finished for him, and he nodded.

'I want to try, Kate,' he said, 'but the big question is do you?'

Out of the corner of her eye she could see the ducks were still swimming round in circles apart from two who had got out of the water and were now waddling away, probably realising that nobody was likely to come and feed them on a cold late October afternoon.

'I suppose we could try living together again,' she murmured, 'see if—'

'No,' he interrupted. 'I mean, if that's what you want then I'll do it,' he added hurriedly as her eyebrows rose, 'but it's not what

I want. I want to marry you. I'm so sure this time that I want my ring on your finger telling all the other men in the world to back off, you're mine.'

'Very Italian macho man.' She laughed, and he grinned.

'You'd better believe it.'

His eyes were fixed on her, and she could see the love in them, the hope, and the uncertainty, just as she also knew that in this man she had found the man who completed her as no other man had ever done, the man she was born to be with. She didn't know what the future would bring, but when she pictured a life without him…

'And we live in the granite house, with the latticed windows, and the country cottage garden, and I learn to garden?' she said with a small smile.

'I'd like that very much, but it would be your decision, your choice,' he said, reaching up to smooth her hair back from her face.

'You know,' she said, 'I think that house might just have sold your proposal to me.'

He blinked, and then his face lit up with a blinding smile. 'Are you saying yes—that you'll marry me?'

'Yes, I'm saying yes.' She laughed, and his lips met hers, taking her breath away.

'There's no way you can take that back now, you know,' he said when he released her. 'I'm a cop, and whatever you say to a cop can be used in evidence against you.'

'I don't want to take it back,' she said huskily. 'I meant what I said, and no way am I ever going to take it back. I love you, Mario Volante, and I'll marry you, which means you're stuck with me. For always.'

'And for always, *amor mio*, I will love you,' he said huskily as he drew her into his arms, and kissed her again.

FREE

4 BOOKS AND A SURPRISE GIFT!

We would like to take this opportunity to thank you for reading this Mills & Boon® book by offering you the chance to take FOUR more specially selected titles from the Medical™ series absolutely FREE! We're also making this offer to introduce you to the benefits of the Mills & Boon® Reader Service™—

- ★ **FREE home delivery**
- ★ **FREE gifts and competitions**
- ★ **FREE monthly Newsletter**
- ★ **Books available before they're in the shops**
- ★ **Exclusive Reader Service offers**

Accepting these FREE books and gift places you under no obligation to buy; you may cancel at any time, even after receiving your free shipment. Simply complete your details below and return the entire page to the address below. You don't even need a stamp!

YES! Please send me 4 free Medical books and a surprise gift. I understand that unless you hear from me, I will receive 6 superb new titles every month for just £2.89 each, postage and packing free. I am under no obligation to purchase any books and may cancel my subscription at any time. The free books and gift will be mine to keep in any case.

M7ZEE

Ms/Mrs/Miss/Mr...Initials ....

BLOCK CAPITALS PLEASE

Surname ....

Address ....

....

....Postcode ....

Send this whole page to:

The Reader Service, FREEPOST CN81, Croydon, CR9 3WZ